THE TITAN CROWN
— PART ONE —

TSHEKEDI WALLACE

The Titan Crown- Part One- Tshekedi Wallace Copyright © 2024 by Tshekedi Wallace

Printed and bound in the United States by Kindle Direct Publishing. All rights reserved. No part of this book may be reproduced or transmitted in any form or by any means, electronic or mechanical, including photocopying, recording, or by any information storage and retrieval system, without written permission from the author or publisher. Exceptions are permitted for quotations embedded in critical articles and reviews about this book.

For information about special discounts available for bulk purchases, sales promotions, fundraising and educational needs, contact:

Edited by S. Jeyran Main
Published by Review Tales Editing and Publishing Services

Cover Design: Flintlock Covers

ISBN: 978-1-988680-46-0 (Digital)

ISBN: 978-1-988680-45-3 (Paperback)

ISBN: 978-1-988680-47-7 (Hardcover)

Chapter One

Grandres Voloxei stood on his balcony, gazing over the tumultuous waves of the green sea in the Bretasi territories on planet Daheza. It was 3091 A.D.E. Having lived for sixty cycles, equivalent to one hundred and twenty years, he found himself in a different era from the destitute times when bloodthirsty hunters and their leaders ravaged many lands. As a young royal family prince in the capital city of Loyanz, before his father's reign ended, he witnessed fleets of cyber-core blackened the skies to protect the cities below. Now, it was many cycles after King Grandres father had died, and these ships, safeguarding the cities of the homeworld, still soared above his palace, controlled by the Mortarsa. They ingeniously utilised the former methods of their enemies, the Giyehe races, from a central hub in the most fortified area of the sacred city of the Kalicos nation. As Grandres allowed the orange-yellow sun to partially blind him, he tracked a sleek vessel cutting through the dawn sky with his red eyes, dreaming of a universe under his command, a vision shared by generations of Kalicos kings before him. Yet, acknowledging that which may be unattainable to him, he settled on conquering planet Daheza as his legacy. Turning away, Grandres re-entered Prince Veleski's royal chambers, adjusting his gown and robes. He extended his left arm, inspecting a coal-black birthmark above his wrist, resembling an ink stain, which he found bothersome. His gaze shifted to his brown skin, marked by small grey spots along his arm and the pronounced elbow bone, distinct from a human's. Observing his peculiar, obese humanoid form, he rubbed his round, chubby face and grunted dismissively. This grunt reflected the indifference of a king unperturbed by his appearance, a ruler who bore his crown with dignity, ensuring his formidable presence was acknowledged by all.

Prince Veleskin entered, momentarily overlooking his formidable father, an action unthinkable for any other Kalicos subject aware of Grandres's powerful reign. Veleskin, preoccupied with his appearance, adjusted a sash over his gown and smoothed his hair. Sharing his father's round, obese physique and distinctive grey forehead dots—a royal lineage trait removed upon ascending the throne—Veleskin scrutinised his reflection for any imperfections. The Voloxei family, known for their beady eyes and susceptibility to ailments, considered health a rare blessing, with Veleskin often using distractions to alleviate his frequent discomfort.

Grandres watched his vain son with amusement and pride, aware of the prince's obsession with his appearance and the widespread tales of his arrogance. The Voloxei were afflicted with a genetic curse, their bodies often appearing diseased, yet positions of power were reserved for those of robust health, chosen from a young age.

Approaching Veleskin, Grandres remarked, "My son, the future great king, I see you're wearing the gown your mother commissioned before her passing."

Veleskin responded, "Yes, Father. I aim to impress our nation's leaders as they deliberate our stance towards the System Lords and the Reduzen warrior race.

All these talks I have been having with my advisors weigh heavily on me. Still, my hands are tied, for we are regulated by the council of Yatavra-System Lords who put us on this planet," Grandres said as he approached his son and with a sad look in his eyes as many of his kind suffered on the smaller lesser planets like Trebaj. "The System Lords have more ships and power and limit our responses in Daheza in our war with the Reduzen to skirmishes in the jungles near our borders. Our small battles have been limited, and none of our galaxy cruiser fleets in space have been used against our enemy."

Veleskin was angered by the facts his father presented to him. He had detested the Reduzen since his youth, spending many solitary nights contemplating commanding intergalactic gladiator legions to war against the enemy, regardless of the System Lords' views. However, he matured and realised the difficult situation his father was facing. "We are being held to ransom. Why? So the System Lords can extort countless Zelcres credits from us for resources we need, laughing as we hand over raw materials from our own lands. Our Kalicos subjects on Trebaj battle the Reduzen scum for control of the planet. They divided our people for a reason, and now they manipulate us by using the Reduzen as pawns. Our kin and theirs are dispersed across several planets, all embroiled in war except for our homeworld, where the most influential leaders reside. The System Lords fully understand our disdain for treating our subjects."

Grandres grimaced, nearly cursing the System Lords excessively, but chose to hold back. He never wanted to waste words. "The System Lords know Trebaj is small and has few valuable raw materials. They regulate us because of our planet's abundance of food, gems, and diamonds. They settled us here to guard the precious commodities they covet."

Veleskin shouted in frustration, "With all the treasures we possess, including white, red, blue, and the newly discovered purple diamond mines beyond our city walls, as well as the gemstone canyons to the east, just past the Kalicos gladiator training camps, our land and treasures are worth more Zelcres credits than the collective wealth of all the younger System Lords, and each of them owns more than one small planet."

Emwefi, the royal court advisor, entered the room. Since birth, his body and face were covered in scar-like tissue. "Your Majesty, they await you in the Hall of Conquerors," he announced. "Wait for us, Emwefi. We will accompany you to the great hall," Grandres replied. Emwefi clasped his hands and bowed slightly. "I look forward to hearing your plans for the System Lords, Your Majesty."

Grandres responded, "We will find a way to satisfy the System Lords while securing what we need."

Emwefi carefully hastened the conversation, aiming to promptly lead the king to the meeting without making it obvious. "Their stranglehold over us seems unfair and cruel."

"They do this to many in this galaxy and others across countless systems, Emwefi."

"Yes, Your Majesty. They target where wealth is found and take what they desire."

Grandres sighed deeply, "We will appeal to them and cleverly provide reasons for their support."

"We have been attempting this for many cycles, Your Majesty," Emwefi observed the king's increased obesity over the last two cycles but concealed his concern.

"I understand, Emwefi. Your impatience is justified, but Fasjey, the murderous Reduzen queen, appeals to them."

The veteran advisor looked sickened by the prolonged discussion about Fasjey. "She believes they will eventually side with her, yet she is deceitful and manipulative."

"That's how she usurped the throne from her sister, my esteemed and honest friend."

"She seduced her sister's husband, then drove her to madness and death, or so it's said, Your Majesty."

"I never grow weary of that tale, a reminder to know one's enemy."

"It reminds us of the challenges we face, great ruler."

"Enough of this. Let us proceed to the great hall for the debate."

Veleskin and Emwefi followed their king out of the prince's royal chambers. At the end of every harvest cycle, the leaders of the Kalicos nation engage in a debate, which invariably concludes the same way. The System Lords either visit the planet to insist on maintaining the status quo for peace or relay the same message from their spaceships.

Grandres can hardly afford to be impatient, yet the Reduzen queen's influence grows among the queens, traders, and warlords who admire her race from other planets. Her capacity to communicate and expand her empire on the planet will undoubtedly garner the attention she seeks from the System Lords, some of whom hold her in high regard. Grandres fears this day might arrive sooner rather than later, compelling him to match or surpass her skills to outwit her at her own game.

Entering the Hall of Conquerors and seeing it as a splendid sight made Grandres sometimes feel happy. The walls, adorned in gold and cream paint, featured intricate black ink drawings of jungle creatures from beyond Bretasi's borders. Turquoise and dark orange gems embellished the walls above the drawings, while the ceilings were studded with blue and red diamonds, surrounded by a silver maze design. This design symbolised the grand gardens of the palace on Zetrax, the original home planet of the Kalicos race's ancestors. They were forced to leave Zetrax following a pandemic that claimed millions, famine, and extensive damage from endless wars, including chemical warfare that resulted in billions of deaths. The System Lords relocated the survivors, a mere fraction of the population. Now, feeling at the mercy of these powerful beings, the king's council reminisced about a time when Kalicos kings, who had once ruled over numerous planets, were not subjected to such control, even after the catastrophic events that occurred their kind.

Within the hall, Grandres observed a round table surrounded by many friends and supporters. However, only his closest and most trusted subjects, including Emwefi, were seated at the table of the blessed ancestral swords. The table accommodated six individuals, with the king positioned. Hence, his back always went towards the door leading to the royal observatories and showrooms, where many historical artefacts were preserved.

Vatemfa, the king's intergalactic gladiator army general, and Palavix, the mentor to the gladiator guard, were formidable Kalicos males. Their muscles and bones, significantly more pronounced than any muscular adult male, required wider chairs than the rest of the advisors at the table. Always battle-ready, their desire for Reduzen blood surpassed all else. They engaged in politics with the fervour typically found in a nation's army's most skilled fighters and thinkers. They were bound by loyalty; the political system linked them firmly to the king, and they trusted his judgment without reservation. Heturadi, the Galaxy cruiser fleet commander, also sat at the table. Tall and slender, he had a long face and an oily complexion. Heturadi was known for his profuse sweating and irregular breathing due to a condition mitigated by the care of the royal protectors' nurses. Rumours circulated that Heturadi was the illegitimate son of the former king, Dowalez. Still, such talk was never entertained by those running the nation. Rising through the ranks, Heturadi earned respect and was seldom criticised despite the fear he instilled.

Anfeku, sitting next to Emwefi, served as the second royal court advisor and Prince Veleskin's mentor. Despite his hideous appearance, marked by facial warts and hand boils, Anfeku compensated with his confidence and charm. Although stubborn, he was unafraid to challenge others' philosophies and knew when to back down.

As Grandres took his seat, touching a sword that, like those for the other council members, pointed towards him, he spoke of the god of conquerors, Seritusu, overseeing their assembly. His ambition was to elevate their nation to unprecedented power, ruling the planet as their ancestors had done on other worlds thousands of cycles ago.

Vatemfa's emphatic table bang, typical of someone commanding the intergalactic gladiators, signalled their growing strength across the system, a fact even the younger System Lords recognised. He decried the System Lords' alliances with depraved beings from a bygone era, used to further their agenda. Vatemfa assured his warriors were prepared for war against the System Lords if needed.

Palavix, visibly growing angrier, expressed his disdain for the System Lords' exploitation of resources from the Borshux mine owners and Wesja traders who oversaw the control of the Zelcres credit system. He cautioned against immediate war, highlighting the System Lords' centuries of empire-building through manipulation and deceit.

Grandres concurred, emphasising the strategic advantage of making the System Lords see the benefit of their power. He reflected on the warrior prowess of the Reduzen and the historical significance of planet Zetrax, suggesting that the System Lords had overlooked the potential respect and admiration for their empire.

Prince Veleskin, standing behind Grandres and known as the rock of Daheza, prompted his father to share their discussion from the previous night about the upcoming harvest festival, indicating his growing focus on his desires over his father's needs.

"The Borshux mine owners have approached me, requesting a partnership to mine the new planets they've acquired through an agreement with Lord Master Hetkarej. I aspire to be a king with boundless resources, as any monarch would. My determination to place us in a position of power across the many systems where our allies and enemies reside is unwavering," Grandres said with a menacing tone. "Although we may not be a nation capable of waging war against the System Lords, who regulate many of our actions and impose taxes, we will continue to grow and surpass Reduzen queen Fasjey Noran. I am committed to reclaiming the Titan Crown once worn by the great king Xathal and others. Hetkarej clings to the crown as if it were his own relic, feeling threatened by the grand history of the Kalicos nation."

Anfeku then expressed his perspective. "We must proceed with caution while maintaining our presence in the jungles and deserts beyond our borders, Your Highness. The Reduzen could strike any moment, and we must be equally prepared to act. We are a race of conquerors, and I advocate invading Reduzen before they can. Invaders claim territory – it's what we're known for, and we should ready ourselves for such actions."

After a moment's contemplation, Grandres responded, "Very well. Prepare to deploy additional Kalicos gladiator battalions to the most perilous zones where a Reduzen attack looms upon my command. We must demonstrate our strength and harbour no self-doubt. The day will come when all I desire is within reach, and we will witness our enemies falter, incapable of rebuilding their empires. Our gladiators will confront the Reduzen generals and Gazaxa beast warriors in the jungles of Daheza and incinerate the desert camps our foes utilise for concealment. The System Lords will not prevent us from safeguarding our borders. Therefore, we shall act without remorse."

Chapter Two

Lord Hetkarej gazed at a star cluster from the open observation deck of his ship, the Yatavra cruiser Eclipse, before his attention shifted to the glass case in the gallery area housing the Titan Crown. He yearned for the era when the Kalicos nation was among the most formidable forces in any system. Hetkarej often reflected on the diseases, genetic disorders, and brutal chemical warfare that had nearly led to their annihilation. Other System Lords believed the Kalicos should have lost all hope of regaining their power and dominance. Yet, one of Hetkarej's ancestors, Ascalo, contributed to the Kalicos's partial rebuilding of their empire, admiring them and having visited the sacred lands of Zetrax, their former homeworld, numerous times. Hetkarej's father, another legendary System Lord named after this influential figure, did not share his son's affection for the Kalicos royal council. Secretly,

Hetkarej aspired to forge a close alliance with King Grandres. However, this ambition required careful, gradual efforts, as most of the Yatavra Grand Lord Masters and Supreme Lord Master Mocowas opposed the resurgence of the Kalicos's former might. Hetkarej's fascination with the history of the Kalicos nation set him apart from his superiors; he wished for their resurgence, contingent on harnessing their talents and gifts under his direction. Such an alliance could augment his influence across all systems, with the Kalicos by his side, commanding respect from many kings and emperors and compelling many System Lords to revere him for controlling the indomitable Kalicos spirit. Hetkarej envisioned Grandres, the formidable ruler of Bretasi, as a battle-hardened leader ready to execute his commands. The Reduzen's sway with the younger System Lords and their influence among veteran lords with Hetkarej's power level highlighted the strategic importance of aligning with the Kalicos, who had conquered numerous resource-rich planets, enriching the System Lords. Hetkarej and his supporters, keen on seeing him ascend to Supreme Lord Master and preside over countless systems, found this prospect enticing. This ambition targeted the position currently held by Mocowas, an omniscient entity with vast resources, who had ruled for over thirty cycles since the royal family's dethronement. Reports of Mocowas's declining health circulated within select circles, revealing his vulnerability. System Lords close to him sensed that his time was nearing its end. Soon, he would meet Axoves, the god all Yatavra beings worshipped, protector of the sacred realm of time and destiny, where the gods observe all beings in creation live out their lives.

    Hetkarej turned around upon noticing that the ship had started moving, gradually picking up speed. He made his way from the observation room to the shuttle shafts, feeling that his time to ascend was approaching. Still, he acknowledged there were other priorities for now. A shuttle descended from the deck he was on, and he stepped in.

"Take me to the bridge," Hetkarej commanded.

The shuttle ascended in the shaft immediately, stopping after just one level, and the doors opened to reveal Ralshefa, the most battle-hardened, formidable-looking veteran female System Lord across any space region controlled by this elite force. Standing tall at 6'3", with long dark hair, tight dark green skin, and dark blue eyes, Ralshefa had lived fifty cycles compared to Hetkarej's seventy. Many System Lords are genetically engineered to govern. Ralshefa had a humanoid, feminine, and slender figure, while Hetkarej was masculine with broad shoulders and a chiselled jaw. His face was long, with yellow eyes. Female leaders are often as tall as their male counterparts, with intimidation playing a significant role in Yatavra training, a trait adeptly utilised by the System Lords.

Hetkarej, struck by Ralshefa's impressive presence, inquired, "Ralshefa, I presume you're heading to the bridge?"

"Yes, Lord Hetkarej," she replied. "I'm eager to be among the first to witness the Grand Lord Master's new fleet. I'm anxious to see and hear their impact on the Borshux miners, inciting fear behind their tall Cetilsun steel doors with whispers of rebellion against the Yatavra race."

Hetkarej pondered the consequences of a potential conflict over the mines with the Borshux chief operator, Desitat, a masterful leader. He questioned the wisdom of risking so many lives for the treasures under miner control, acknowledging the alignment of the miners with powerful races beyond System Lord's control. This diminished their political authority over the lands operated by the miners and sparked debate over the distribution of major resources, with miners seeking to retain more.

"I, too, am keen to see the new addition to the galactic fleet," Hetkarej stated abruptly, "To the bridge, immediately."

The shuttle carried the two Yatavra- System Lords up three decks to the bridge. Upon arrival, they were greeted by the sight of the Eclipse crew, standing in awe of the Grand Lord Masters' galactic fleet. Unlike typical cruiser fleets, these ships were monstrous in appearance, rectangular yet square at both stern and bow, painted a dark grey. Enormous laser cannons, mounted on huge turrets above and below the bridge and three and four-barrelled cannons capable of 360-degree movement promised remarkable accuracy. Additional cannons lined up on high turrets towards the stern. The bridge was visible at the front, though observation screens were blacked out to conceal the crew. Similarly, the observation deck screens were obscured.

Each battle cruiser in the fleet could carry two hundred and twenty Yatavra fighters, surpassing the capacity of cruisers used by each Grand Lord Master. The small, heavily armed vessels aboard these ships featured a distinctive square design with a small cockpit and a roundish pointed end, coloured white and dark green. The main cannons, almost half the length of these vessels, were mounted on the sides. Every cruiser bore the Yatavra crest, a crimson serpent with slightly curved yet sharp white fangs. Hetkarej admired the sight before him while Ralshefa pondered the fleet's potential uses. The fleet comprised five hundred and seventy battle cruisers, each led by one of three veteran System Lord commanders, built for durability and power.

These cruisers were exceptionally fortified, boasting more heavy artillery than any carrier cruiser. They ranged from multi-barrelled laser cannons to long-range missiles, ultra-pulse-wave mines, and bombs that could be launched from space just above a planet.

The communications officer turned to Hetkarej, "Lord Master Hetkarej, Grand Lord Master Gorxab is requesting a communications link from his ship, the Darkseed."

"Accept his request and put him on the viewscreen," Hetkarej commanded.

"Yes, sir," the officer replied, pressing a blue button on the communication system's touchscreen.

Gorxab Jowekre, an overweight, pompous, and vain individual, prioritised only his family, a few friends, and his wealth. A former Yatavra prince, he wore his royal garments whenever possible and seldom ventured beyond his palace unless necessary. His siblings showed no interest in becoming System Lords, preferring the luxury of a few of Etrehen's palaces, served by male servants and maids. Despite King Loheyal Jowekre's overthrow and the disbandment of the royal family, they retained the admiration and respect of many Yatavra citizens. Mocowas believed they required oversight yet should appear content and well-treated. Gorxab had contributed to his father's dethronement, who was then confined within the white spiralled tower of the fortress of metal thorns, which, to the public eye, resembled more a palace, leading citizens to believe the king lived contently as a hermit.

Hetkarej addressed Gorxab informally, "My friend, the once lonely prince who lives as no king ever did."

In Hetkarej's circle, formalities with Gorxab were often overlooked. Despite many heads of state retiring after the fall of the post-royal family, Hetkarej remained well-connected and enjoyed their favour. Mocowas had warned him, concerned about his popularity, but Hetkarej, undeterred by the possibility of overstepping, remained defiant. Mocowas, recognising Hetkarej's defiance and potential, knew he was a skilled leader backed by many of Etrehen's elite, including Gorxab's family.

Gorxab laughed heartily, "Ah, my cunning lord master of the three systems, where the Mortarsa breeds their hybrid army from the genes of other superior warrior races, now dependent on your charity. Your dealings, including with me, are admirable." His eyes gleamed with malevolence as he considered his next victim to exploit. He took pride in the Yatavra's hybrid and cloned armies' widespread deployment across thousands of planets. "I've heard you've generated unprecedented Zelcres credits for Mocowas and presented him with mines filled with jewels to honour his reign. You're keeping the old legend satisfied. My family, once royalty that was never opposed and ruled over all Yatavra citizens and many other races, now known as Etrehen's gatekeepers, observe closely, anticipating the day you ascend to Supreme Lord Master—a topic freely discussed among closed ranks."

Despite his desires, Gorxab knew acting against Mocowas was futile. Hetkarej's strategic positioning ensured his advantage as Gorxab loved him as a dear friend and confidant. At the same time, Mocowas, though no fool, wielded unmatched power, rendering opposition foolish in the eyes of even his detractors. Hetkarej grinned but quickly adopted a serious expression. "Perhaps it's wiser not to discuss such matters openly, Gorxab. Mocowas doesn't always take things lightly. He becomes slightly agitated by this kind of talk. It is he who decides his successor and no one else."

Gorxab bellowed with laughter once more. "The choice is clear, Hetkarej. Revel in the anticipation, for you will undoubtedly be the chosen one. There's a reason why no Yatavra lord we've dealt with dared to challenge you when you proclaimed you would herald a new era for our kind. No being could surpass the current great king of the Kalicos nations as you have. Not even the first System Lords, who forged our homeworld, Etrehen, possess the strategies you've employed to temper the fury of Bretasi's brute and his son, ensuring they never reveal their desire for vengeance against us. Grandres owes his vast empire to you.

He's gained favour with many thanks to your allowance for his growth. He would do well to remember that."

Ralshefa smiled wickedly, appreciating Gorxab's remarks on control and strategy.

"Lord Gorxab, please, join us aboard," she said. "Why communicate via viewscreen as if we're short on time? Let's discuss matters in the command quarters, where significant decisions are made. We'll await your arrival to discuss the nations we must tax following our territories' next series of harvest festivals."

Gorxab, laughing heartily, clenched his fists. "Those territories are numerous, Ralshefa, but still insufficient for me. I won't rest until we've negotiated with every dealmaker, bargained with every trader, and regulated all possible planets with our fleets and armies to secure food supplies for our race and offer security to many—at a price." He chuckled again. "In these challenging times, it's better to be safe than a target for any of our so-called allies, who, given the chance, would exploit those weaker than themselves."

Hetkarej glanced at Ralshefa, whose eyes sparkled with enthusiasm for Gorxab's vision of a perfect system.

"We await your arrival, Gorxab," Hetkarej said. "Bring the other Grand Lord Masters. We'll enjoy fine Yatavra wine from your palace vineyards and feast on boiled jerefi spider eggs until we're sated."

Gorxab licked his lips. "I'll be there in no time. Have the wine and my favourite delicacy ready, and I'll supply the reweska sea serpent meat for our feast. As the god Axoves would say, my kin has been good to me, so I must dine with them, sharing the knowledge that empowers me, even in the darkest moments, to guide the masses through tumultuous times."

Ralshefa observed the crew, inspired by Gorxab's words.

"There's much to be done to sustain our breeding colonies and citizens on Etrehen and across our system indefinitely," she noted. "Our armies and fleets expand, requiring financial support for our engineers to acquire all the Cetilsun ship metals needed. We must continue striving to be the ultimate rulers, ensuring we're never overthrown by our so-called allies, many of whom wish to see us fall—"

"And let's not forget those who silently observe, waiting for an opportunity to scavenge from the aftermath of any conflict," Hetkarej added. "Overcoming our forces won't be easy; we must remain strong throughout."

Gorxab stood and moved forward. "We've always monitored those around us. This conversation via the ship's communication system has lasted long enough. I'll come to you. Be prepared for my arrival; it won't be long. Then we can delve deeper into our current standing compared to those who whisper of a world without the Yatavra race and speculate on who would dominate in our absence."

Tshekedi Wallace

Chapter Three

The courtyard of Queen Fasjey Orunvo's main palace in the Panonetes territory was breathtaking, featuring white marble floors and black walls adorned with pillars painted in golden yellow and cream. Sunlight streamed through the antique treasure gallery roof windows leading to the court. Dominating the palace grounds was a black pyramid-shaped structure towering over its surroundings. Beyond the palace's front lay tall white pillars and solid brown walls of varying heights, while lilac towers at the back housed the queen's female guard. These guards, known for their ferocity and animal instincts, were legendary across systems familiar with Reduzen history and the beast wars of the past, which caused a massive loss in their race numbers. The Yatavra offered them sanctuary under their protection on Daheza, but at a cost. Now, they paid a tax on everything they fought for and owned.

Fasjey stood in the gallery, eyeing each jewel of historical significance she now possessed. Her sister was dead, and she had ascended to queenhood. The events had stirred the royal court like a sudden storm. Fasjey loathed the gossipers, finding their chatter as distasteful as the stench of death lingering on a battlefield. The three royal palaces housed many elite society members, accustomed to a life of luxury and decadence, who whispered of Fasjey's hatred and alleged murder of her sister, Leywenel, and her love for Leywenel's husband, Swalok Ternor, now residing in Panonetes' second-largest palace. Despite their mutual attraction, Fasjey and Swalok maintained a pretence of separation, even though they were in love. Fasjey, seen by some as a murderer, believed her actions were necessary for the empire's survival under her rule. She plans to marry Swalok eventually, but it is too soon since Leywenel's death.

Fasjey's gaze lingered on the necklace Leywenel had worn in death, not wishing to dwell on the poison that had seeped from her sister's mouth. Fasjey, the orchestrator, and Leywenel's husband witnessed the act involving venom from deadly desert spiders found between Panonetes and Bretasi. Fasjey justified her actions by her sister's cruelty.

Turning, Fasjey noticed General Jarkepe approaching in his black combat suit adorned with purple holsters for his laser guns. The general, embodying the Reduzen race's humanoid and beastly characteristics, was the most formidable-looking Reduzen male. With wide, slightly swollen eyelids, dark purple pupils, and rough, tar-like black skin, Jarkepe epitomised Reduzen traits, including pronounced jaws and thick, muscular bodies. Reduzen males rarely had hair, unlike the hair-bearing females, and both genders possessed thick, claw-like nails.

Fasjey, with her grey/brown hair and wide face, shared the green eyes common to queens in her bloodline. Her teeth, sharp in front and half blunt at the back, were mostly white, though some had yellowed. A lover of sweets, Fasjey anticipated her maids' afternoon treats in the queen's pink tower's private kitchens. She planned to whiten her teeth and diet with the harvest festival approaching. She desired to look her best in robes made from the softest materials and long multi-coloured scarfs.

Jarkepe's perspective had significantly shifted after the System Lords granted the Bretasi territory to the Kalicos, diminishing the clear advantage the Reduzen race previously held regarding land on the planet. Bretasi boasted extensive grazing lands essential for feeding animals. The Reduzen craved Parokavax meat, a brown creature resembling a cow that matured rapidly. Although this food source was abundant, the queen, her general, and their race were unwilling to share any resources with the Kalicos, their adversaries who would eagerly consume every resource owned by the Reduzen queen.

The Reduzen nation once ruled Daheza until the Kalicos were relocated there, becoming sworn enemies known across many planetary systems as cruel invaders with ambitions of ultimate conquest akin to their worshipped deity. The System Lords had entangled Fasjey and her race in a divine game, claiming many nations in what they called defence. The dark queen felt more like a slave under an evil master's guidance than a ruler sovereign over many.

Jarkepe bowed slowly, inquiring, " Your Majesty, my one and only queen, how has your day been?"

Fasjey strode past her general into the garden beyond the courtyard, reflecting, "I smell the flowers my garden keeper planted under the burning sun of this cycle's first quarter when the star shines so brightly that no Reduzen dares to tread the stone pathways of our cities during the day's first half. I ponder over the lands we could reclaim from Grandres. I dream of seeing flowers in the gardens of many palaces I would construct as I govern my people, thinking of my warriors trampling the ashes of vanquished Kalicos gladiators."

Jarkepe, inhaling the fresh air infused with the sweet scent of aqua-coloured flowers, never tired of this sight within the palace courtyards.

He then expressed, "I, too, yearn to gaze upon the graves of numerous Kalicos gladiators, Your Majesty, to witness their blood painting the walls of every city they settled in so many cycles ago. Mocowas should have abandoned them on their refugee planet. Grandres thinks he's destined to rule all, but he's mistaken. No commander has ever subdued the Reduzen on our soil. Vatemfa believes his intergalactic gladiator legions can defeat the Gazaxa beast warriors, but this city will never fall. We control our destiny and will nurture masters for every generation. The formidable Reduzen warrior race will stand unyielding; the warrior god Hojoval will ensure it," Jarkepe declared, his tone intensifying.

Fasjey, continuing through the courtyard, surmised, "So, you too believe Grandres's invasion is imminent."

"Yes, great one," Jarkepe confirmed. "Our beast army stands ready, ever-prepared for war, aware of the threats we face. Let Vatemfa's forces come; we shall vanquish them all."

Fasjey's wicked smile conveyed her resolve. "Ensure our victory, Jarkepe. We are not mere worms to be trampled. I am determined to expand this nation and reclaim our rights should we be attacked, regardless of Hetkarej or any System Lord's directives."

Jarkepe harboured a deep-seated disdain for the System Lords, thirsting for war and relishing the kill. The thrill of the hunt was paramount, and with thousands of hunter cruisers spread across many systems—and secret allies aiding their expansion—he anticipated playing a pivotal role in a war to end all wars.

"My queen, a feast is being prepared before the harvest festival."

"Jarkepe, my faithful general, this feast only serves as a reminder of the vast food supplies the System Lords require to sustain their armies and Yatavra citizens across their dominions."

Jarkepe, seething with rage, learned of Hetkarej's mandate from the Grand Lord Masters to leverage their abundant food supplies to coerce nations with starving warriors into their ranks, bolstering their military might.

"I will inform Oshdan to take as much territory as he can until you inform Hetkarej of your decision to aim for peace, Your Highness. I am sure this will fool him for the time being. There is no end to your genius, and you have the most powerful mind of all the royal subjects on this planet and any other world that exists, great queen."

Jarkepe bowed his head and walked away from Fasjey towards the first set of palace gates that were fifty feet tall. He was looking forward to giving his beast master the order to be more ruthless and severe as his beast army attacked with one last group of assaults in his quest to take more land before the queen contacted Hetkarej and carried out her plan. Jarkepe knew the queen would still wait for quite some time before she contacted Hetkarej. Things would fall in their favour due to the dark-minded queen's genius level of intelligence. He was sure of it.

Chapter Four

The land overseen by the intergalactic gladiators on lookout duty was desolate under the cover of a dark, foggy night on planet Trebaj. Visibility was nil as they manned the watchtowers of their vast, fortified encampment. Tasked with guarding the most formidable terrain, the gladiators were thinly dispersed yet had managed to reclaim some territory in recent days.

Positioned with their sharpened claws gripping their laser guns, two hundred Gazaxa beasts stood ready, their shoulder blasters aimed towards the gladiators below the hillside across a vast field of brown and green grass. Their expressions were fierce, their resolve to fight until their last breath unmistakable. They donned silver, black, and cream armour embellished with the golden Gazaxa claw crest on their thick metallic breastplates.

Unaware of the looming threat, a battalion of Kalicos gladiators assembled in the camp on the other side of two large hills. Displaying their malevolence, they stamped their feet with force, sharing with their leader their deadly intentions. They spat on the ground, urinated on the floor and engaged in raucous laughter as they fired their guns into the air, illuminating the night sky with laser blasts. Some gladiators, wielding long laser spears made from black Cetilsun metal with sharp, protruding laser blades, beat their chests and shouted Grandres's name. These spears, capable of inflicting deep, gruesome wounds, were a hallmark of the gladiators' arsenal, necessitating mastery despite their infrequent use in combat. After a display of aggression, they discarded their spears, showing signs of restlessness and irritation in their pathrak skin uniforms, the material sourced from a rough, big-boned, six-legged creature native to the muddy lake banks of Bretasi.

The battalion was led by a formidable 7'5" gladiator mounted on an Orekesi beast, a gargantuan four-legged creature with hardened green skin reminiscent of a rhino in bulk but with a round head distinguished by an unusual bone structure and a cluster of bumps near its ears.

The orekesi beasts, with their short dark snouts, snapped their gnarling sharp teeth as they reared their heads, displaying large hooves surrounded by brown hair.

The battalion leader, a gladiator of imposing stature, had a wide chest and unusually developed muscles on his lower body, while other areas appeared slightly chubby yet distinctly masculine. His skin was dry, marred by warts and boils, and adorned with green paint streaked diagonally across his face from forehead to chin. His Mohawk-style hair was greasy and dark.

He tugged at the reins, turning to observe seventeen other gladiators who struggled to control their orekesi beasts amidst the cold weather, making them more agitated. The creatures emitted a high-pitched scream, a natural-sounding call among their kind in the jungles of planet Eregahi, their origin. Like many battle creatures, orekesi beasts possessed advanced senses and emotions, making them valuable in combat.

The commander shouted, "Guard, open the gates. The orekesi beasts crave the cold night air."

Upon the gates opening, the gladiators, armed and ready, rode out into the misty night. Though the fog slightly impaired their vision, they trusted the lookout's vigilance and the orekesi's keen senses to navigate the darkness.

As the orekesi charged into the night, their heads thrashing until restrained by the gladiators, they crossed the hills rapidly, their riders spurring them on with the metal heels of their boots. Reaching the top of the second hill, the commander, momentarily lost in thought, was struck squarely on the jaw by laser fire, his face disintegrating upon impact. He tumbled from his beast as chaos ensued, with laser fire exchanged between the gladiators and the Gazaxa beasts. The battlefield was littered with flesh and bone as some orekesi, panicked or injured, caused further casualties among their riders as they fell on top of them.

The sounds of ambush reached the camp, prompting the activation of three laser cannons mounted on tall grey metal poles, ready to defend the over five hundred warriors and one hundred and fifty orekesi beasts within. The forthcoming clash with the Gazaxa promised to be a fiercely contested battle, remembered and recounted as a significant event among the inhabitants of Trebaj.

The Gazaxa beasts charged, unleashing laser fire at the gladiators manning the watchtowers, eliminating them from their positions. As they advanced, gladiators stationed at the camp's perimeter returned fire. Still, the dense fog rendered their efforts futile against the more accurately firing Gazaxa. Amidst cries of pain and the triumphant roars of the beasts, it was clear the gladiators were at a disadvantage, outmatched by their adversaries' strategic positioning and aim.

The gladiators, operating the cannons remotely from a control tower distanced from the camp, watched as the cannons uprooted huge chunks of earth with their wide laser blasts, sending some beasts airborne. A Gazaxa beast, distinguished by a long horn hanging from a silver chain around its neck, blew into it forcefully. The piercing sound reverberated, accompanied by the growls of several hundred beasts in the distance. This prompted the gladiators to retreat while still firing their laser guns, seeking cover behind the camp's front barriers and cannons.

As the Gazaxa beasts advanced, firing their lasers, those gladiators not fully shielded by the barrier were hit. Despite knowing the beasts had a superior sense of location due to their keen instincts, the gladiators continued their counterattack.

Approaching closer, some Gazaxa beasts revealed missile launchers on their backs, unleashing missiles at the cannons and destroying the heavy artillery in a relentless assault. The camp's structures, including the control tower and living quarters, were also struck by laser fire.

The battalion leader rallied the gladiators behind him, some wielding dual laser guns, and encouraged, "Charge with your brothers in arms, and we will see this through to the end."

As they engaged, the Gazaxa beasts, adept at evading laser fire by moving on all fours, lunged at the gladiators, slashing at their legs with claws. The gladiators fought back fiercely, biting or shooting at the attacking beasts, who continued to assault the Kalicos fighters, inflicting scratches and drawing blood. Many gladiators, having shed their full armour earlier in revelry, were more susceptible to injuries.

Surrounded by these formidable opponents – the only kind the Reduzen queen and general would deploy – the gladiators were overwhelmed. Despite their valiant efforts, they were outmatched, with veterans falling as if they were novices.

The victorious beasts, mocking the fallen invaders, executed them with precise shots to the head. Following this, the Gazaxa warriors moved to eliminate any remaining orekesi beasts, leaving none for the Kalicos to discover.

The horn-blowing beast signalled, using the loud instrument that made a sound that moved the Gazaxa beasts emotionally, summoning three Reduzen warriors atop tethaza beasts. These formidable creatures, resembling black lions with prominent red horns on their heads and white tusks resembling an elephant with a far sharper end, approached the scene of triumph. The creatures started to pick at the bodies of the gladiators who lay on the ground, ripping the flesh off their corpses. Oshdan, the Reduzen beast master riding one of the tethaza beasts, commended the warriors, "You have done well to defeat these gladiators. I will report to our queen that we anticipate capturing more land in the coming ten days through relentless assaults from air and land. The Kalicos, now fearing us more than ever, retreat to safeguard their major cities, leaving the smaller ones vulnerable to our conquest with minimal resistance. Be prepared for the next offensive, but remain vigilant. The gladiators' retreat is strategic; they are formidable foes. Once you have further assessed this land, join us in our territory. Make haste to safety."

This strategic victory highlighted the ongoing tension and the shifting power dynamics on the planet as both sides prepared for the relentless struggle for dominance. Oshdan turned and rode away before the Gazaxa beasts could respond, swelling with pride for his finest warriors. The beastmaster was content, knowing he had secured the advantage. Now, he prepared to meet with the queen, eager to recount his victories and anticipate her reaction to his achievements. As the appointed beast master, much was expected of him, and he was well aware of how the queen despised failure and expressed her anger. The possibility of frequent losses was not something he could afford.

Fasjey's penchant for tales of the violent demise of Kalicos's most formidable fighters was no secret to him. Thus, Oshdan planned to regale her with numerous accounts of the battle and assure her of his unwavering commitment to their cause. He intended to convey his determination not to cease the onslaught until Trebaj and Daheza were unequivocally theirs, leaving no room for opposition.

Chapter Five

A fleet of one hundred and eighty Borshux ships, each carrying one hundred and fifty fighters, approached several large fleets of combined renegade forces of various races. These forces had claimed a colony of planets rich in raw materials and minerals. Chief Operator Desitat, the Borshux leader, coveted these valuable planets for his own empire. Conquering them from the renegades would impress the Yatavra-System Lords, whom he felt obliged to appease for now. Sorzikel, the Borshux Miner's Federation Fleet Operations Master and commander of the flagship Black Hammer positioned his fleet behind the moon of the first planet in a small system. The ships, featuring round bridges and square middles with robust, thick hulls, were designed for durability, their rear adorned with high beams flanking the propulsion system. Laser cannons were strategically placed in the middle of the vessels, with missile platforms and bomb launchers equipped for territorial scatter bombs, utilising ultra-hyper-sonic pulse wave technology capable of devastating a planet's surface.

Sorzikel, a temperamental yet calculated Borshux, surprised his crew with the intensity of his anger, given his thin, seemingly frail humanoid physique. Despite his unhealthy appearance, marked by bald patches and peeling skin, Sorzikel was agile and quick-witted, attributing his fitness to liaisons with females of various races, a pastime he joked was the only exercise a wealthy Borshux needed.

On this pivotal day, Sorzikel selected the best fleets under his command to demonstrate to Desitat and the Yatavra that he could annihilate any renegade resistance, thus earning rewards and more lavish indulgences. As a regent of vast cities on conquered planets, Sorzikel enjoyed immense wealth and influence, ensuring the loyalty of mine bosses on his home planet, Otreven, by keeping renegade control at bay.

Meanwhile, Ikizuni, the Jekaxtu captain and a leader among the renegade forces aboard the flagship Ravage, steeled himself for the battles ahead, determined to defend his newfound home against the Borshux and Yatavra. Ravage, a fearsome battleship converted from a storage vessel, boasted extensive missile capabilities and speed unmatched by others of its size, a testament to the ingenuity of Cetilsun engineers and Mortarsa builders who had built the ship to be incredibly sturdy when it travelled.

Ikizuni, straddling genius and madness, had proven his prowess in battle, ramming Ravage into enemy flagships and outmanoeuvring his opponents. Aware of the looming threat from the miners and the System Lords, Ikizuni was prepared to fight to the end, refusing to submit to exploitation and heavy taxation.

Reflecting on his unique heritage and the strength it bestowed, Ikizuni acknowledged the challenges faced by the Jekaxtu, a race decimated by war and disease yet resilient in its quest for survival. Despite being the most pursued among the renegade races, the Jekaxtu's struggle for existence continued as a testament to their determination and the legacy of their genetic ingenuity.

The pirate scavenger crew aboard Ravage chanted, "The Hecaz race is here, the Rotumze race is here, the Noxret race is here, and we'll fight until the new horizon is upon us when we will be free of the evil Yatavra race." The ship's advanced communication systems were activated, allowing the same rallying cry to echo through the other ships in the renegade force. In near unison, every being across the one hundred and seventy-five vessel strong fleet joined in the song. Ikizuni felt a swell of pride as both a leader and a warrior. War would erupt at dawn on the planet he now called home, transforming the darkness of space into a spectacle of light, stirring his spirit. He adjusted the sleeves of his uniform, crafted from vibrant, fireproof, and blade-proof battle fabric, then positioned himself steadfastly beside his chair.

Sorzikel concluded his contemplation of victory. "System controller number three, release my attack vessels into the void. We shall triumph and, after that, mine these lands. I am the fleet operations master, serving only the chief operator and the Yatavra, for we dominate over lesser beings. My day will come."

The appointed systems expert activated several controls on a touchscreen and then elevated a holographic bar that materialised before him, nestled among dot-like sensors with a thin glass pane framed by wire-like metal strips above, displaying the ships' power source energy levels. The bay doors of every vessel in the Borshux fleet swung open.

A fiery sensation engulfed Sorzikel's stomach, a hunger kindled by his fondness for vetacav meat, a boar-like creature with pot-bellied, blue/grey skin that nourished over three billion Borshux citizens on

Otreven. This inner blaze signalled his need for nourishment. Yet, Sorzikel knew better than to issue commands on a full stomach during the conflict. The Borshux digestive system, prone to producing loud, distracting noises post-meal, could not interfere. With the Borshux attack fighters poised for engagement, Sorzikel resolved not to order a retreat, seizing this chance to vanquish the renowned Captain Ikizuni.

Ikizuni observed hundreds of attack fighters advancing from beyond the moon towards his new homeworld and commanded readiness for defence against the impending assault.

"Let it be recorded that on this day, we were compelled to take lives solely to survive and secure our freedom. Let our fighters engage and repel these invaders, the most despicable across all galaxies. Bridge crew, prepare yourselves." A bridge crew member activated the bay doors of the Ravage by pressing a button on a holographic projection emitted from a delicate glass screen with underlying sensors. Seventy-five small fighters launched from the ship, bearing the heavy design of Jekaxtu engineering intended for ramming as a final act before a valiant demise. Their prism-shaped structure, complete with visible metallic beam landing gear, was complemented by side-mounted laser cannons and newly fitted propulsion systems, enhancing flight smoothness and safety. As these aggressive pilots united with other renegade forces, they commenced a barrage of laser fire. The ensuing close-quarters combat resulted in significant casualties on both sides. The renegade fighters specifically targeted the small front viewscreens of the Borshux attack vessels while the Borshux sought to dazzle their foes with bursts of flame and light, deftly manoeuvring at high speeds to evade the Ravage's laser cannons. Despite their robust construction, the round Borshux fighters with pointed ends and double-barrelled cannons couldn't withstand the Ravage's overwhelming laser fire.

The flagship's bridge weapons specialists unleashed their rapid-fire laser cannons with relentless fervour. They maintained their ruthless campaign to eliminate all Yatavra allies, regardless of their stance on combat for the merciless System Lords. Despite their agility, some Borshux fighters were struck down, disadvantaged by the overwhelming numbers as the fleet operations master pursued total victory.

The broader conflict saw the renegade fleet's fighters deeply engaged, with their green laser beams intersecting the Borshux's red fire. Both sides scored hits, reducing spacecraft to flaming wreckage or fragmented debris obstructing other vessels.

The renegades' zeal sometimes led to premature strikes, missing their intended targets and suffering the consequences of counterattacks. This desire for revenge revealed a merciless nature, as not only the intended enemy but also many innocents perished due to the conflict's ferocity.

The battle appeared relentless, yet the ferocity commanded by Ikizuni's fleet presented a novel challenge to the Borshux attack fighter pilots. Each fighter possessed unique advantages, influenced by their origin. The Noxret flagship and its supporting fleet bore designs reminiscent of the gowang, a predatory pet from the Noxret homeworld, embodying stealth and puma-like attributes. The cruisers' sleek, elongated forms featured cannons strategically placed at every corner of their high, terminating edges. These vessels combined formidable firepower with exceptional speed, equipped with quadruple cannons on turrets arrayed across the wide nose end and with the bridge positioned closer to the midsection. Their distinctive purple and brown hues, adorned with African-inspired patterns in yellow, red, and green, symbolised the chaos of space combat life with the colours representing fire, blood and growth. At the same time, black lines with white star motifs paid homage to the Noxret's storied journey through space and time.

The Noxret fighters, among the smallest close-combat assault vessels, exhibited a high stern and a sleek curvature towards the front, where the pilot's cockpit was flanked by two humps just before the dual laser cannons, including a fast-spinning turret for targeting passing ships.

As the Jekaxtu and Noxret fighters united, the Hecazy carriers and Rotumze cruisers surged forward, noticing the Borshux fighters' preference for confrontation. Sorzikel, intent on eradicating as many renegades as possible, remained indifferent to his fleet's losses, with Ikizuni being his primary target as per Yatavra's directive.

The Rotumze cruisers, with their unique flying axe-like appearance, featured a partially curved and rectangular brown front, resembling a handle extending towards a pointed, axe-like end with flaps. Double-barrelled laser cannons and revolving missile platforms adorned the ship's length, requiring skilled pilots for operation. The Rotumze flagship, Soul Seeker, mirrored this design on a grander scale, equipped with numerous missile platforms and a large crew for territorial engagements.

The Hecazy carriers, with their imposing, monstrous design, featured bulging ends with side flaps on the stern. The larger nose end supported three major bridge sections within the ship's expansive, triangular midsection, embodying both might and majesty in the renegade fleet.

Gigantic laser cannons adorned the ship's body, prominently featured along the top and bottom of its head-shaped nose and stern. The Hecazy fighters, prism-shaped vessels akin to Jekaxtu's, boasted super-powered laser cannons arrayed along both sides, ready for close combat. The carriers and fighters displayed a green, brown, and dark red palette. The Hecazy flagship, Carnage, earned the moniker "the ghost maker" for leading the formidable thunder fleet, named for the lightning-like appearance of their cannon laser fire emitted from the long five-barrelled lasers positioned across various points on the ship. The fleet's prowess instilled fear in their adversaries, securing their long-term survival within the renegade force.

The Rotumze broke formation, luring the Borshux attack fighters into their trap before systematically destroying them with precise shots from their revolving cannons, exploiting the enemy's disarray to strike from behind.

As the Borshux forces were compelled to split, the Hecazy fighters, organised into three groups resembling a hurricane, penetrated their ranks. Comprising both attack and scout ships capable of long-distance raids, the Hecazy pilots demonstrated exceptional discipline and mental resilience, fundamental traits of their race.

United, the Hecazy and Noxret fighters, with the Jekaxtu in support, executed a tactical encirclement. The Rotumze circled to ambush the Borshux from the rear, delivering devastating blows. Sorzikel, witnessing the obliteration of his forces as the renegade fleet decimated the Borshux attackers with intense laser fire and cannon assaults, closed his eyes in resignation.

Upon seeing the Borshux attack fighters engulfed in flames and his fleet's inevitable defeat, Sorzikel commanded a retreat to hyperspace, leaving the battlefield to the victors. The renegade forces celebrated their triumph. Ikizuni relished the victory, ready to bolster his fleet's numbers for the planet's defence. Acknowledging the miners' potential return with Yatavra's support, he remained steadfast in his commitment to protect his home and forge alliances to counter any threats. Ikizuni envisioned his domain and surrounding space soon bristling with ships poised to safeguard what he cherished.

Chapter Six

The Giyehe leader, the prime architect Dekrehas, who had a long face with pale grey skin, faded yellow at the top half of his ears, and a pot belly, walked with a slight limp due to undergoing a surgical procedure. He chose not to use his walking stick as he thought it would be seen as a weakness, and he recovered quickly without any aid. The Giyehe mastermind looked presentable in a cream robe with a light teal sash. Dekrehas made his way through the new temples of Kretaq, the planet where he had ruled for five cycles. He entered one of the beautiful structures and saw that the temple's smooth marble floors, painted moon white and a gentle peach, were so clean they sparkled in the daylight. Elders walked around the temple dressed in fine silks, admiring the structure as they ascended its long stone steps with golden arches above them. The walls inside had copper-coloured drawings depicting the first great architects who built their civilisation of creators and constructors. Tables and chairs, made from the strong trees that were hundreds of cycles old and could be found in the great forests of Kretaq far beyond the safety of the capital city, Atroxat, were placed in the corners of the temple and along the walls. Beasts lurked in the woods, and the constructors and labourers who built for the architects risked their lives to obtain the wood for their work. The doors were plated bronze; temple guards in red uniforms stood every few metres.

Dekrehas was a leader who knew his kind was constantly under threat because of whom they had chosen to be their allies a long time ago. The Reduzen had helped the Giyehe when the System Lords in their region of space had decided not to support them in a long and brutal war with a faction of miners and traders that had banded together and formed the almighty galactic miner's union, which was eventually disbanded. This had happened before Queen Fasjey's time. However, the Reduzen ruler knew that Supreme Lord Master Mocowas wanted to be the power that dictated to the Giyehe for his own purposes. Still, he could never be a System Lord who negotiated how the Giyehe should do business with him on any level. The Giyehe were so powerful that the System Lords could not extort a ridiculous amount of Zelcres credits from the mighty race, the most important universal form of payment in many systems. The Giyehe still paid a tax because their ancestors had said it must always be paid, as every race was a cog in a well-oiled machine as far as they were concerned. The System Lords protected countless civilisations spread over vast distances in space. They had helped to build legendary empires.

The Reduzen beast armies and the Star Ranger fighters had taken substantial territory. More than five million of the hardened, focused warriors were on twelve planets, and far more were due to be sent to assist the occupying force. They were being bred and trained exponentially on breeding colonies in other systems that could not be regulated as pirates and scavengers had controlled these regions of space. They never bothered Fasjey's forces much. Five space stations and three gigantic space docking yards had been captured, and the enemy's ships were being stripped. Shipyards were being used as mega border patrol bases to regulate the regions around the planets the nations now shared. The Kalicos armed forces allies, the Mortarsa builders, were at war in space with the Giyehe and the Reduzen. The System Lords would not intervene, and this bothered Dekrehas greatly.

The Kalicos armed forces and the allies they fought with were an undeniable threat. Hetkarej had given Grandres several diamond and food-stock-rich planets. The king was forever grateful to the cunning System Lord, but this had been a scheme to make Dekrehas feel threatened. A war ensued, which the Kalicos fleets won, with the help of mercenaries as Grandres refused to commit his full space force in battles that were a distraction from his other problems, which the Giyehe fleet commander Paltovis never saw coming. Now, he had eight more planets with more food and raw materials than usual due to their size, which needed to be mined. This meant that the miners wanted to work with Grandres and formed a union strengthened by the support of the king's allies. Grandres held more weight with Hetkarej in the process even though the System Lord knows both Grandres and the Borshux miners sought to break away from the grip of the System Lord's council. Hetkarej had thrown the brute of Bretasi a bone, and it had made the king ten times more powerful, necessitating a reconsideration of his position in the scheme of things. The System Lords rarely give those who could question their dominance an opportunity to survive their wrath. However, they favoured the Kalicos because of their history and former strong relationships. This gave Grandres an advantage over Fasjey, who, whilst having some support from a few Yatavra geniuses who help run certain parts of the empire, threatened many of the System Lords more than the calculated king. This fated history occupied the prime architect's mind every waking moment of the day. Soon, the Giyehe fleets would be embroiled in a war to end all wars, and he feared the Reduzen hunter cruisers would be spread thin unless he could build thousands more quickly. Ultimately, the System Lords were bound to want to stop any major war between Dekrehas and every one of Grandres's allies to control the narrative for all involved. Dekrehas felt that there was a chance the Giyehe could be facing the Yatavra, the most powerful force in any system, if they chose to eliminate the Kalicos threat, no matter what. Fortunately, more than half of the Giyehe's allies would support them if they went to war with the System Lords. The renegade forces would join the Giyehe in any battle against a common enemy, so they knew other nations not yet in league with them might join the war against Mocowas. Many wanted to see his timely demise.

Dekrehas walked past the statue of the king of the gods, Vahirites. They observed as the constructors' families prayed for their kin to make even greater creations. The part of the city near the temple had traditional old-looking buildings with designs inspired by the old cities that existed when the gods' offspring were said to have roamed amongst the Giyehe race. There were beautiful sky blue and pink towers and light grey cobbled streets with smooth black paved roads and large sandy brown stone huts with pale red steps around the back, leading to large gardens with rainbow-coloured flowers. Beyond the structures outside the temple, the highly advanced architecture was mostly grey and white, with shuttle tubes throughout the great city, taking citizens everywhere they needed. The buildings loomed like endlessly tall skyscrapers, partly covered by an almighty dome that lasted for miles, covering the main part of the city, with the outskirts being uncovered. Only security ships could fly through the massive gaps in the dome, an almost impregnable metallic shield.

Tadrushi, the graceful temple caretaker and Dekrehas's wife, walked into the temple with several guards. She was the prime architect's pride and joy. Nobody mattered to him as much as she did. Tadrushi smiled and approached her husband, gazing up at the statue of Vahirites until he noticed his only true love and showed her affection. The Giyehe were a race that was never afraid to let others know how they felt publicly. Although a few males and females in positions of power were slightly averse to showing affection towards their partners in front of strangers, Dekrehas and his wife were not among them. The wise ruler placed his hands on Tadrushi's shoulders and gently kissed her on the cheek. She caressed his face with her left hand, like a wife who always responded to her husband's show of affection without fail. Some of the other Giyehe smiled, then looked up at their god's fifty-foot statue, ensuring they appeared in awe of the dark grey stone carving. The statue depicted Vahirites in his long robes as he stroked his beard. He held the book of the realm lords, who were the advisers to the gods, in his hands. The Yatavra believed the realm lords gave their ancestors the visions that made them the leaders they were.

Tadrushi held her husband's hand, and they walked through the temple into a prayer room with smaller statues of Vahirites. There were Giyehe citizens everywhere, and they muttered prayers to themselves as they knelt on embroidered mats.

Tadrushi walked closer to Dekrehas as they approached her private rooms. "My darling, how will you deal with the attacks on our fleets by the Mortarsa cruisers and fighters?"

"Elazret, that demon fleet commander. They call him Stone Heart, and he never stops, Tadrushi, my love. We must rely on fleet commander Paltovis to protect our borders."

"We are losing Giyehe pilots daily, and the citizens are very concerned," Tadrushi said as she pushed her hair to one side. Her body was humanoid and mostly muscular like her husband's, but she had slim legs, soft blue skin, and strawberry-blonde hair. Tadrushi's eyes were a lighter shade of hazel/green, her eyebrows were thin, and her open face looked welcoming. The loyal partner of the prime architect was shorter than her husband and wore white boots with red heels that matched her white and red robes. Tadrushi spoke softly in a tame manner as she felt her husband would respond better, "Even now, our pilots have regrouped near the base station in the Yutumek system. Then we have the patrols protecting the space near the planets where the newly built Reduzen hunter cruisers have gathered."

"We have a vested interest in those planets. The land taken from Grandres's allies has abundant raw materials, and the Reduzen share the spoils of war with us," Dekrehas said.

"Husband, I want you to build more Giyehe ships, as you said. Our engineers and constructors are working too slowly. We must pick up the pace to keep up with the allies of the nations we helped the Reduzen to conquer as the Mortarsa attack us regularly."

Dekrehas responded to his wife in a raised voice, "We will soon deal with them." He stopped his temper from flaring and smiled. "The allies of many of our enemies have the support of the System Lords for now. The veteran System Lords do not want the Reduzen queen taking too much territory. Because we do not cower when Mocowas and his bullies speak, he will intervene if we strike down those who oppose us without using smart tactics. We will react like an offensive menace at some point, Tadrushi, just not for now."

"We must wait until the time is right. Then, we will take down the System Lords for good and be free of all tyranny. Dekrehas, that intergalactic political thinker, my brother, the citizens' voice, waits for me in my private room. Let's go and see what he is doing."

"Ah, the philosopher," Dekrehas said. "I do enjoy conversing with Razcet. His heart is pure, and his mind is always clear when deciding with the city architects. His travels always take him somewhere adventurous."

"He complains about the long distances he has to travel to see new worlds sometimes, but he is happy," Tadrushi said.

"Razcet knows he must find influences for the cities we are going to build on other planets we will get from Queen Fasjey," Dekrehas said. "He is important to us all."

Dekrehas and Tadrushi walked through a see-through curtain leading into a room where temple servants prepare sweets of all shapes and sizes to be eaten after prayers. Food and wine sat on white tables along the walls of the room. The couple walked into a private prayer room and then stepped through a silver and pink-coloured curtain that was made from the most beautiful tribal race materials, which was before a doorway leading to a study with books and scriptures on shelves and counters. Razcet had his back turned as he read from scripture. Tadrushi walked forward, and Razcet turned around. He had a wiry, almost gaunt-looking body, but his cheeks had a little colour. Razcet had the passionate look of a Giyehe politician and trained architect, always ready to speak about the issues. Razcet had bright brown eyes and pasty-looking skin on his hands. He wore sandals, a black toga, and a white gold ring around his neck on a chain. It was his late wife's ring that she gave him to keep when she was on her deathbed before she was laid to rest.

"Sister, you look wonderful as usual," Razcet said. "I was looking through some of our history. The architects of the past have been so formidable it exhausts my mind just thinking about the best way to equal them."

Dekrehas grinned. "You have seen a vision. Now, you look to the past to see if you can match the originators of our style and craft, Razcet."

Razcet smiled as he slowly interlocked his fingers in front of him. "You know me well, brother-in-law. In my heart, I feel the nation's pulse pushing me to improve, which makes me ambitious and gives me an incredible rush of energy like nothing else. Legacies help inspire others to build the city's strong foundation, and the citizens take anything that inspires them and then look to the future, seeking to aim for the stars. This is a part of the belief system our culture has had for thousands of cycles. They believe it will help them in the afterlife. A gift that will stay with them for all eternity."

Tadrushi embraced her brother and said, "Razcet, I cannot wait to see what your constructors have done. Soon, they will finish building the new city, Epeyi, where the most significant temple on our planet will sit in the city's centre. Once it is finished, it will be a joyous occasion."

Razcet pulled away from his sister and looked towards the scriptures. "I am focused. Time is not on our side due to past wars that have created more enemies for us to battle with. I must leave you now, and I bid you farewell. May the rest of your day be fruitful." Razcet nodded slightly toward the prime architect, who felt proud of his brother-in-law's work ethic, then walked towards the doorway.

Tadrushi and Dekrehas walked arm in arm towards a pair of tall, cushioned chairs shaped like small thrones near the shelves straight ahead. Before they sat down, they gave each other a passionate kiss. They knew their love had no bounds and would be that way forever. The prime architect and his wife believed that if their bond remained strong, it would help the Giyehe, as all could see this as an example to follow. They lived to serve, and not much came above that for the two of them. Dekrehas had a lot to protect, and soon, his moment would come when he would have the opportunity to lead the Giyehe race to greatness.

CHAPTER SEVEN

Elazet, the Mortarsa fleet commander, stood on the spacious open bridge leading to the bridge crew's observation room and private galley. The flagship Blood Vengeance hovered above Mortarsa's home planet, Srekaz, with an impressive fleet of four hundred cruisers and carriers and hundreds of close combat attack vessels patrolling the area further away from the planet. The twenty-five-stone-strong man was tall with long arms and big hands. His arms were behind his back, and he sneered, which caused his heavily scarred face to look even more ugly. The Mortarsa features were still apparent, and his brown face with three orange streaks down the front of it looked severe as the thoughts of a true menace entered his mind. Elazet's nose was half flat and half bumpy. It looked as though it had been broken twenty times. His skull bones protruded through the thick brown/green skin on his head. The fleet commander wore a brown battle fabric combat suit covered by a red blazer with commendation badges.

Elazet thought about the imminent attack that was coming his way. He looked at the ship's Captain, one of the countless captains who got on board the flagship Blood Vengeance to get an opportunity to become a crew member; also, an overweight Mortarsa male nodded. The Captain waved his hand sideways in the direction of the ship's pilot, and the ship moved forward slightly into a more defensive position just behind fourteen cruisers that were also moving slowly.

The Captain walked forward up to the long-view screen and said, "Commander Elazet, there are sixty more cruisers on the way and by the time the battle begins, we should have one-quarter of the Mortarsa fleet waiting not far from our position, and they are more than ready to fight, sir."

"That will have to do," Elazet said. "The rest of the fleet is protecting our interests from the Reduzen queen, who uses her ships to raid and attack us wherever we are vulnerable. Fasjey is rumoured to be on the verge of building more ships. We already have many ships but need to add to the fleet. We must be ready for Fasjey and all who follow her."

The Captain looked determined to see an end to the threat that faced them as Elazet did. "You are right, sir," he said. "As the Mortarsa builders, it is part of our duty to kill the enemy of King Grandres, take everything they hold dear to them and destroy it in front of the eyes of those who fought beside them until they all shudder. They will become whelps who fear they will suffer the same fate if they continue to oppose us."

Elazet walked up to the Captain and stood next to him. "Each time we approach the Yatavra to ask them for help in these space battles, they tell us this will cause an escalation of warfare among the races. Still, they have a new fleet of cruisers made for space battles of a satanic proportion.

A young gung-ho System Lord told me they are building even more in the Ketewdi system. They have the biggest shipyards in any system, and many ships constructed already have a crew. Soon, the Yatavra-System Lords will be too hard to beat."

The Captain looked eager to have his say but hesitated as Elazet stood still and pondered what lay ahead.

"Grandres waits patiently for an opportunity to make Mocowas hear his voice. As far as he is concerned, if he does not get his own way, he does not get to wear the Titan Crown," Elazet said. "The masterful king feels Hetkarej is taunting him. Grandres is an effective analyst and thinker who knows when his time is wasted or when a being is playing games with him. There is no scheme he cannot see before it comes his way, but many want to see him controlled for the rest of his days. Fasjey, along with many others with the same contempt and hatred when it comes to the king who wants to conquer lands, is eager to see his life get extinguished."

"I agree with everything you have said, Fleet Commander Elazet," the Captain said.

Elazet sighed heavily, then said, "We have taken many lands using Grandres and Vatemfa's battle plans. I believe soon he will want to collect, and we will have to fight all who oppose Grandres with him in an almighty war. I still pray Mocowas supports us in any war against our enemies, even though we are strong allies of the Kalicos race. Still, I am sure many will have to decide whether to fight against or support the System Lords one day. They are no fools and will be watching everyone while ensuring that any war they have does not weaken them to the point where they get defeated by those who wish to see an end to their reign, which in this era is absolute. Kalicos is a king who wants their blood as he does not like to be seen as the pet of the Supreme Lord Master."

"I am glad that I was picked to be the Captain of Blood Vengeance, the greatest flagship of its kind, for this battle, Commander Elazet. I know many have had this role, as we are a race with more than one war hero to take positions of superiority on any vessel. I thought I would never get the chance."

"Let us both hope, captain, that this battle is a good one, as we know there is a planned attack, and I hope I will see you again after this," Elazet said.

Before the Captain could respond, Elazet walked away, approached the observation room, and looked through a view screen longer than the bridges. The flagship was an incredible beast, and building it was remarkable. It looked like two ship-like towers connected by another long, thick tower between them. The vertical rectangular towers had square blocks at the top, and cannons were lined up in a row from top to bottom. Wall-to-wall security team rooms were in the towers, along with private quarters for the crew, medical centres, armouries, and escape hatches for emergencies. The long horizontal tower consisted of the bridge and observation rooms, the commander's war gallery, the bridge crew command centre, and the captain and commander's ready rooms. Elazet was proud of his mega cruiser. Whilst it did not have attack vessels on board like the old model flagship Retribution, it was a ship that could more than hold its own and be a death-defying opponent in any battle. It could do major damage to a fleet of average cruisers by itself.

Forty cruisers came into plain view. They flew at a snail's pace towards Blood Vengeance. Twenty more went out of hyper-light speed further away from the planet. They moved into position and lined up in a row. They were cruisers built solely for blocking any attack with pure laser cannon and missile power. The ships had as much weapon power as the famed Rotumze cruisers.

A communications analyst called, "Captain, I'm receiving a message. Cruisers are being attacked in the Powetos system not far from here."

Elazet became alert. "The enemy has chosen to attack us closer to home rather than distract us by attacking our ships and space docking stations further away from home and attempting to get us to send our ships to far-off destinations."

The Captain's face held an expression that told Elazet he had thought victory would be something they could celebrate without losing many lives. "They know we have protected our bases and border patrols close to other planets where Mortarsa will work and live in the future."

"I am not fooled," Elazet said. His face was just as serious as ever, and he wanted to see the death of hundreds before he closed his eyes on Srekaz at night when he lay down to rest. "They will attack those places even more one day with our king living on the planets if we cannot protect our home on this day. They risk being surrounded by this desperate attack that makes no sense. We control so many systems in regions of space around our planet. Tell all other ships to be ready for a full-scale assault wherever they are. The Reduzen hunter cruisers and Star Ranger fighters may not be in this battle, but her allies are formidable. Today, we fight the Lutresas empire. They were called the war breeders before many other races throughout time because they use the most violent psyche technology methods to prepare the minds of their clones for when they must confront the enemy. They are a heartless race when they fight on land. Just like a beast queen to befriend the wildest animals she can find."

Close combat vessel pilots were ready to risk their lives. Attackers flew at speed towards the planet. Three hundred attackers flew to the left and right of many of the cruisers and hovered there while the other attackers stayed in front of the ships. Another eighty-five attackers came out of hyperlight speed further away from the cruisers spread far apart.

These attackers flew all around the area they were in, back and forth repeatedly. All the close-combat assault vessels were green and black. The cruisers, including the Mortarsa flagship, Blood Vengeance, and the old flagship Retribution, were green and black with a yellow stripe across the towers, while the cannons were white. All the other mega-cruisers had a similar look. The communications analyst touched his ear and said, "The Lutresas fighters have wiped out our line of attackers in two systems, and we are under pressure in the Hortrax system. We are being asked to send as many reinforcements as possible."

Elazet walked over to the communications section of the bridge. "Call our spaceport in the Radarek system. Get them to send half the attack fighters that are there to support those who are in the Hortrax system. Do it now! Ready yourselves soon; the Lutresas will come to us, and we will make them see only flames and blood!"

A whole fleet of cruiser ships arrived. It was the heathen fleet, so-called because of the behaviour of the crew used to run the ships. A mercenary breed of Mortarsa warriors who lived in the jungles of Srekaz when they were not in space. They were all directly related to the tribal Mortarsa, and they never allowed their warriors to converse with Mortarsa, who had bred with other races and was a member of the other allied nations. They had demanded that as a show of strength, the Mortarsa should fight with as few outside forces who were allies for as long as they could when protecting their own planets. Elazet had agreed, as he had no choice. The heathen fleet fought in the most brutal battles, and their war chiefs and the commanders in the seat of power on Srekaz had an unorthodox level of knowledge. They were among the greatest minds on the planet.

There were one hundred and forty ships in the heathen fleet. Half were cruisers that carried some attackers with highly experienced pilots who were decorated veterans on board, and half did not have as many experienced pilots but were expertly trained in space and ground combat. The cruisers that did not carry attackers had more laser cannons than any vessels in any Mortarsa fleet. Their only purpose was to destroy as many enemy close combat attack vessels as possible. These cruisers' enormous laser cannons could target fighters from a long distance away. The gigantic vessels simply looked like an X with a square as a frame. The ship's structure had cannons lined up, and down the vessel almost everywhere the eye could see, which only left space so the cannon's turrets could operate. The bay doors could open in the corners of the ships. The bridge was in the cruisers' middle section and was heavily shielded.

The bay doors opened on the heathen fleet cruisers and the attack fighters that are based on designs that many allies were given because of a deal that was struck aeons ago when the Mortarsa were a less powerful nation until the Yatavra realised the potential the race had to grow and wanted to use their skills to design and re-build cities that had been decimated by war for their allies on other planets. The genius vessels the Yatavra created for others were used by races in systems so far apart that fleets of cruisers in outer space that had never met each other would recognise the designs and technology being used as a Yatavra blueprint when they scanned each other's ships. The attack fighters looked like smaller versions of the cruisers, with a square in the middle of the vessel where the pilot was and heavily armed wings that were pointed at the end. They looked jagged where the missiles were kept.

There would always be ships available to defend Srekaz. The planet also had six hovering cannon stations half the size of space stations. They were always ready for action. As expected, the crew on board the stations were experts at using laser cannons and anti-gravity torpedoes. Even though they were top veterans, they had to train in simulators continuously while on the homeworld.

The attack fighter ships of the heathen fleet flew farther ahead than all the cruisers and other close combat vessels protecting Srekaz. These legendary warriors were the first line of vessels the Lutresas would meet in battle. Elazet had decided to use them because they fought hard and made the fight seem endless no matter where it was. The commanders on Srekaz had prepared the armies for an invasion, knowing that anything could happen. But it was suspected that this would be more like an attack to test the defences of Srekaz so the Lutresas's military superiors would not send an invasion force.

Suddenly, Lutresas fighters came out of hyper-light speed and flew straight at any fighter close by, firing their blue lasers and hitting the target. But the heathen fleet attackers had pilots on board who craved combat and feared losing so close to home without having a say. They drove the Lutresas fighters back with the heathen fleet's cruisers laying down covering fire.

Two hundred and fifty more fighters came out of hyperlight speed. Elazet looked at the fight that ensued and saw flames of white that flickered and then burst, making balls of explosions that looked like orange fireballs, causing smoke and mist to rise with light around them. This made Elazet want to see his pilots be the victors. The Mortarsa carrier's bay doors opened, and their pilots flew out of the massive docking bay decks in large groups in an organised fashion.

A large group of heathen fleet attackers flew high, and the attackers directly behind them shot the Lutresas fighters down ferociously. The laser fire blitzed the cloned pilots before they could even react. The attackers that had ascended dived and fired on thirty-two separate ships that had just come out of hyperlight speed and shot their wings off, damaging the main structure's mechanics. The Lutresas's wings were long, and their ends looked like an eagle's beak.

Laser cannons were positioned underneath the wings. Three small cannons were aligned in a row on either side of the fighters' strong oval main body. They were fast and difficult to catch in a chase.

Lutresas battle cruisers appeared just as the heathen fleet was utilising their ship's laser cannons to their full advantage against every one of the fighters that emerged from hyperlight speed and could not manoeuvre quickly enough to evade them. The grey and blue ships were long and rectangular, with an oval section in the middle where the bridge crew piloted the vessel and oval-shaped weapons hubs at each end where missile platforms and laser cannons were located. Sixty-five had arrived, with fighters launching from a quarter of them as the Heathen's fleet cruisers fired upon the long-wide Lutresas vessels. The oval weapons hub cannons on the Lutresas ships repeatedly fired on the Mortarsa close combat vessels. Then, they launched a massive array of missiles at countless cruisers, targeting only the weapons systems and parts of the ship with lesser shielding. All the Mortarsa vessels had heavy shielding around parts of the ship, controlling the main operating systems used for flight and environmental control. The weapons systems on the cruisers had heavy shielding on some ships where the weapons systems were located but less on some models that were faster and lighter. These ships suffered as the missiles struck them, causing them to explode and drift sideways and downwards as the Lutresas fighters finished them off.

There was a high probability that the Lutresas would lose the battle they were about to engage in. Fasjey and the ruler of the Lutresas nation, Queen Xunaseta, agreed completely on most matters. The Yatavra had relocated weaker alien races it had dealt with over hundreds of cycles for their own purposes. Fasjey, like her allies, wanted to harm anyone who opposed their plans to make themselves formidable opponents that Mocowas could never question. The Supreme Lord Master was so preoccupied with building an incredible empire that grew daily exponentially and herding other races in different planetary systems while dealing with renegade forces that there was a chance for Fasjey and any ally to take advantage of all the distractions that the System Lords were dealing with. The main plan was to bomb military strongholds of Srekaz and destroy space stations that the Mortarsa commanders could not afford to lose. Loss of life was expected to be high by the two queens, but it was worth the risk to test the enemies' defences.

More Mortarsa fighters arrived; the battle was like a combination of a tornado and a hurricane. The Mortarsa fighters mostly moved to the beat of the Heathen's drum. When the domineering pilots attacked, the other lesser Mortarsa pilots would support them, and the Heathen's cruisers provided covering fire to the battle cruisers with fewer laser cannons.

The Lutresas were advancing as their near-suicidal fighter pilots combined their forces and distracted the heathen fleet cruisers until the Lutresas cruisers could focus the firepower of three cruisers on the heavily armed Mortarsa vessels. The ships illuminated each other, and shielding scattered everywhere in large chunks. Elazet knew there was a good chance that Blood Vengeance and Retribution would not be safe from the attack even though they had now repositioned themselves near the cannon stations. No Lutresas fighter or cruiser had breached the Mortarsa defences, but that was about to change.

More Lutresas vessels arrived. They were coming from the attack on the space docking stations where Mortarsa ships had been awaiting orders to battle elsewhere against other enemies, and docking stations with ships were being repaired or waiting to be taken to the shipyards. All the Mortarsa vessels at the space docking stations had been destroyed.

Elazet stood on the bridge and readied himself. "Order our cruisers to leave two routes for the Lutresas fighters to get through where our cannon stations can pick them off and take them down. Tell the cannon station commander to start firing as soon as our ships are clear and leave them with a window of opportunity."

The Captain nodded at the communications analysts. The young, excited Mortarsa crew member pressed the touchscreen before him. He leaned forward and spoke clearly over the panel next to the touchscreen, with a small holographic sensor near a speaker system device and the other ship controls.

"To Commander Tatshal of the heathen fleet," the analyst said. "Clear a route that will deceive enemy vessels. They must fly into the path of the cannon stations. Coordinate with the other cruisers from the ship Retribution and her fleet."

The heathen fleet's response was almost immediate. The vessels separated while still firing heavily. As the ships separated, they converged on Lutresas cruisers already heavily fired upon by Mortarsa attack fighters. The advancing heathen fleet cut off the Lutresas fighters, protecting their cruisers as they were attacked. As this happened, a gap was left where the heathen fleet cruisers once were. The former flagship Retribution and the fleet she fought with moved slowly to help the heathen fleet fend off the attack from other Lutresas cruisers that came to the aid of their fleet vessels. As they did, a second gap was left in the Mortarsa defences. Lutresas fighters converged and flew through the gap at high speeds, but so did three cruisers. The larger vessels were far slower, but they were surrounded by over two hundred fighters that took on laser fire as much as they shot enemy attack fighters out of the sky, protecting the cruisers. The cannon stations sprang into action. The laser cannons fired rapidly. Lutresas fighters pulled up and dived to avoid being hit by the large laser fire, but some pilots didn't even get a chance to get near Srekaz. The laser cannons on the other side of the station shot down many of the fighters. Still, some got away and headed for the planet, descending quickly. Their shielding was specifically designed for entering into the planet's atmosphere, ready to attack. An erratic array of laser and missile fire blitzed the three cruisers that got near the cannon stations. Their noses pointed downwards as they started to explode, and their onboard operating systems failed.

Other Lutresas cruisers emerged from hyper-light speed at a distance. They saw what was happening and immediately joined the fight just as another five mega-cruisers, almost twice the size of a normal cruiser and mainly designed for lengthy space battles, emerged from hyper-light speed, and their bay doors opened. Hundreds of fighters filled the space around every Mortarsa vessel in sight. The cannon stations acted and targeted every fighter attacking Mortarsa vessels being fired upon. Elazet understood chaos, and as Blood Vengeance started to fire her weapon, he realised that the Lutresas knew that his enemy desperately wanted the upper hand and had been meticulous and smart about their battle plan.

Two cannon stations fired heavily upon seven Lutresas cruisers, firing every missile in their arsenal at the stations and immobilising some sections of the defence systems. The gigantic cannon stations still had too much firepower for the cruisers to get through. However, twelve more cruisers attempted to push through the heathen fleet, with over five hundred fighters having close combat space fights in their vicinity. They aimed to take down the Mortarsa attack fighters. They killed more pilots than the Mortarsa battle commanders could afford to lose.

The Heathen's fleet became ultra-predatory. Some flew at a distance at their fastest impulse speed and shot down as many fighters as possible. In contrast, others created a blockade before the ship's Blood Vengeance and Retribution to protect them. Then, the last of the heathen fleet joined some other Mortarsa cruisers and cut off as many Lutresas fighters from attacking the cannon stations and getting past them to approach Srekaz and attack the military facilities on the planet's surface.

For the pilots, the space battle no longer seemed like a fast and furious fight. The laser fire sometimes went nowhere near the vessels being aimed at, and then they would hit a ship that happened to be flying close by. The friendly fire caused many deaths. The first set of fighters that broke through the planet's defences had gotten through just as more Mortarsa vessels from space stations at some of the furthest distances in light-years away from Srekaz had arrived. They shot down Lutresas fighters like they were nothing. These Mortarsa's main fleet ships were designed to be ultra-destructive vessels, and the heathen fleet vessels and their laser cannons packed more punch. The impact from the cannons was horrifying as they made the fighters they fired on change trajectory immediately. The massive firepower that killed pilots made others lose control and hit other ships as they tried to avoid being fired on repeatedly.

The fighters that had reached the planet's surface had their targets in their onboard computer systems, and they launched a heavy laser cannon attack on the enemy on land. Most of the battle command facility defences were especially advanced with Artificial Intelligence defence systems that needed no crew to control them. The facilities, with a crew of Mortarsa controlling weapons, fought with hate and temper in their hearts and minds. They were merciless and shot as many fighters down as the AI cannons did. No Mortarsa being could be seen, not even in the cities, as they were inside or underground. Bases that did not have Cetilsun metal plating covering all the vital structures were damaged.

Lutresas cruisers broke through the Mortarsa defences and got smashed by the cannon station fire from the front. As the Mortarsa cruisers regrouped, they were hit from behind, but hundreds of fighters still got through. The cannon stations did their worst and destroyed the cruisers' weapons hubs, then crippled the cruisers with the help of the Heathen's fleet ships that had not been too badly damaged from a heavy barrage of missile fire from the Lutresas cruisers that came out of hyperlight speed. The last lot of Lutresas cruisers emerged from hyperlight speed. More carriers with bigger, closer combat vessels had a complement of missiles on board for another attack on the planet among the ships. These ships were long, wide, and high, but they were rectangular and very long to carry as many fighters as possible. They opened their bay doors, and the vessels looked like a sea of ships ready to come in waves with only a heavy assault on the cards for the enemy.

There were still plenty of heathen fleet vessels that were fully functional, with a few more ready to put up a fight if needed. The rest had parked themselves in front of Retribution and her depleted fleet to stop any fighters from taking them entirely out of the equation in a heartless fight.

The Mortarsa cruisers that had fought the least in the battle had to prove their worth, and they jumped into action. They fired heavily on the Lutresas vessels and were fired upon by ten vessels at a time, with fighters getting through to meet the wrath of the crews on board the cannon stations. At least four large groups of fighters from the last assault, with over one hundred fighters in each group, got past the cannon stations. The cannon stations' unstoppable laser attack obliterated the rest of the fighters.

The fighter pilots who had broken orbit knew they were possibly flying a suicide mission as they could hear on the radio that not many would return to Qukosi to see their queen hail them as heroes. The heavily armed fighters got to the surface and fired their missiles, looking to cause maximum casualties. Top secret military installations were underground, but many of the military bases on Srekaz were fired upon as the pilots dived, hoping they were killing at least some military staff they knew had killed their brothers and sisters in arms. The military cities where the Mortarsa armies lived and trained were fired upon next. The buildings caught fire, and the sun's heat helped the flames stay alive. The commanding officers were treated like royalty on Srekaz. They protected the builders' interests and properties. They safeguarded future projects by keeping plans secure and ensuring any unions the builders made with other races were upheld with cunning tactics and genius know-how for being convincing and helping build foreign relations. The Lutresas pilots knew they were underground, so this time around, the ruthless superiors would not be killed.

The AI defence systems did their worst, shooting down fighters two or three at a time. The Lutresas that were hit did their best to smash into any important structure they could. The cannons took down most of the fighters by the time they reached the fifth military city of eleven. The Lutresas pilots had done their best, more than the Mortarsa had ever thought they could. They fired their last missiles on the cities, ascended, and flew away from the planet.

Elazet watched the weapons station crew members pick off enemy fighters left, right, and centre. The cities on his planet were attacked by some well-trained pilots one minute; then, in an instant, they were using their hyperlight drives to take them away from the madness below. The heathen fleet cruisers were shooting fighters as they passed them. Others that were floating aimlessly were destroyed with a single laser shot. Elazet knew he had been outsmarted to some extent. The Lutresas forces had done a lot of damage, but he also knew he would most likely be commended because his fleets fought well. He had proved he was a formidable commander without giving many orders because his crew's training spoke for itself. He was a master, and he would tell the other commanders on Srekaz that one of the most ruthless races that the Reduzen queen had made her allies could not hinder them and had suffered far more significant losses than the Mortarsa fleet, which was something to be recognised.

Chapter Eight

Prince Valeskin walked through the yellow and blue painted hallways leading to his father's private chambers. He knew Grandres would be waiting for a call from Mocowas. The king had a feeling of disdain for the all-seeing System Lord. Valeskin wondered how long his father's patience would last, for he was calculated. Still, he was under pressure from other members of the family who were close to him. Kalicos' royal court subjects were whispering like they always did, and many agreed that the Reduzen would soon get the upper hand because Queen Fasjey's forces were becoming more aggressive away from planet Daheza.

The Yatavra had too much experience in the ways of war, control, dictatorships, and politics to be ignored or brushed off with simple talk. They had the final say on many things. Grandres was trying to angle his way into gaining the trust of the higher circle of System Lords totally and completely before finally betraying them. They were unaware of his planned schemes, and he wanted to keep it that way. He wanted no upheaval or disagreements between him and Hetkarej, even though he dreamed of Vatemfa's forces crushing his skull.

Valeskin entered the king's private chambers through the silver double doors. They were grandiose rooms which had been designed with opulence in mind. In the king's main quarters, the curtains were sea blue. The ceiling had a painting of the Honturad nebula close to the former Kalico's home world, Zetrax. The painting consisted of a beautiful mix of colours that looked like turquoise and purple. The floors were cream, and the walls were painted cloud white with a silver tint at the top and bottom just below the ceiling and above the floor. Grandres sat on a large seat made from the finest wood of the trees, far beyond the Bretasi territory's borders. The Reduzen queen had waged a large military campaign, and a large region that was heavily protected had been regularly attacked. Still, the king was stubborn and wanted to take more space away from his enemies slowly. He realised the skirmishes he had sent his gladiator battalions to get involved in had lasted for half a cycle. Still, he was determined to take as much ground as possible while protecting his own gem canyons. This made Mocowas upset as he felt Grandres and Fasjey were being defiant. Still, the king was defending his right to his land, and Fasjey would say she owned it at one point.

The Reduzen general Jarkepe had sent many cloud gliders on the long journey to the gemstone canyons to attempt a major assault on the workers and gladiators that protected the area. The Kalicos cyber core attackers had been defending the area heavily and had been successful in many respects. Still, the attacks were becoming more frequent, and

Grandres was getting concerned. Mocowas wanted to speak to him about this matter and other things.

Valeskin sat opposite his father. The chairs were a twin set made by Grandres's cousin's carpenters. The chairs' intricate design was why Grandres always sat in them, with the carvings on the armrests of the chairs of the jungles of Daheza being beautiful. Valeskin was tired, but he remembered his father's teachings about the duties of a future king, never stopping even if one is worn away and quickly shrugged off the tired feeling.

Valeskin spoke openly, "Father, I had hoped to sit in on your meeting with Mocowas. I want to see what he says about how he intends to deal with the space battles over the last cycle. We have been fighting this war with the Reduzen here on Daheza and far from home."

"You can stay but say nothing, Valeskin."

"Yes, father."

Grandres looked at the sky outside the window. "It is approaching dawn."

Valeskin follows Grandres's eyes. "Mocowas rises early to have his meetings. He expects kings to serve his every whim."

"The world is very different for Mocowas than us, but the tide will turn eventually, my son."

"Yes, Father. This time in our lives is frustrating, and I want us to see an end to the war between us and the Reduzen so you can focus on getting the Titan Crown on your head where it belongs."

"The time will come when we'll speak about the fact that we were planning for the day when we have no more lands we need to conquer as we conquered them all," Grandres said as he stood up and walked over to the wine cabinet. He picked up a bottle of wine and turned around.

"On that day, you will see a Titan King with a kingdom that stretches far and wide. The empire will grow, and other civilisations will worship us."

"We will never crumble under pressure, and a thousand empires will follow us, great king."

"No king, queen, or emperor that fears me will act without my blessing, Valeskin, prince of

Dahezaa, you will inherit the great throne of the Titan Kings."

"The throne of spears will see many great kings sitting upon it. I look forward to the demise of the System Lords and all who believe they should rule."

Grandres looks at the wine in his cabinet and takes out a bottle. "Servant, come in here!" he said loudly.

A young servant dressed in white robes with a grey sash around his waist enters the room.

Grandres speaks to the servant forcefully, "Make sure you get many bottles of this wine from my cellars. We will fill our glasses and be merry when we feast tonight."

The servant took the wine bottle and replied, "Yes, Your Highness." He walked out of the room and shut the doors.

As soon as Grandres sat down, a sensor in the wall in his quarters beeped, and he stood across from it. The sensor scanned him once, and then a holographic projection of Mocowas appeared before him. The Supreme Lord Master looked almost regal, which was amusing for Grandres and Valeskin, particularly because he had wanted to wipe out the royal family on Etrehen for many cycles before they were made useful in a different way so the Yatavra citizens would not rebel against the System Lords. Mocowas was a tall male who stood 6'8" and loomed over all the Yatavra System Lords. He was the most powerful System Lord of his kind by far and had superseded the power of every lord who had held the position before him. Mocowas's eyes were red, and his green skin looked a little darker than the Yatavra race's skin, usually due to his age, which still happened to a few of the older cloned System Lords.

Mocowas was a masculine and imposing figure. "Hello, King Grandres," Mocowas said. "How are you?"

"I am fine, Supreme Lord Master Mocowas. However, I predict my gladiator legions will be under pressure if I do not retaliate here at home and far away from our shores on planets in other systems."

"Keeping the peace on Daheza is vital," Mocowas said. "Make your presence felt, and we will speak with Queen Fasjey. We will warn her that any more attacks will warrant punishment from us. But what happens on this planet is not the real problem. Both you and the warrior queen have been waging war on other territories using your own military, and you have been getting your allies involved. It seems that you have been taking advantage of the fact the Yatavra are under pressure out here in the darkness of space where I now spend most of my time."

Suddenly, Grandres looked to be uncomfortable in his seat. "The renegades bring war and uncertainty to the doorstep of the miners and others. After the battle between Fleet Operator Sorzikel and Ikizuni, who is now rumoured to be the fleet commander of the renegade force. The enemy you face has grown more confident."

Mocowas smiled. "We have almost doubled the new fleet, and more ships are being built. These renegades must not think of us as weak. This is how fools falter. You must stop this war with Fasjey. The System Lords have no time to deal with the old scores you feel the need to settle. Your deal with the miners also means you risk being attacked by the renegade forces. You have bigger things to worry about."

"Fasjey is now adding to her fleet using the Giyehe engineers. I have already told you I suspect this is happening on a massive scale. The Lutresas have attacked us and our allies for a full cycle and have not stopped for a fraction of time. Their ships attack us and kill countless pilots. Twenty-three border patrol bases and space stations combined have been destroyed. I have not heard of Queen Xunaseta being reprimanded by the System Lords. I must respond, so I have ordered my fleet commander, Heturadi, to launch a full-scale attack on the Lutresas planets and all their main strongholds. My intergalactic gladiators will rip through their ground defences once the galaxy cruisers have done their worst."

Mocowas's mood changed. "Listening has never been your strongest trait, Grandres. If you attack Qusoki, the Lutresa's home world, there will be severe repercussions if the ensuing war interferes with the business my System Lords have between the traders and the miners on planetary systems that Queen Xunaseta controls. You have already distracted the Giyehe with your petty skirmishes over territory. Take this issue further at your own behest. You have been warned, and as I told you, I will have words with Queen Fasjey about this problem you both have with one another. I must go now. I sense you have much to discuss with me, but I am being urged to deal with another matter. We will speak again soon. Goodbye."

Grandres looked at Valeskin as soon as the Mocowas hologram disappeared. "After Heturadi and Vatemfa are successful, we will have the harvest festival. Our defences are impenetrable, and we have more cruisers in space than most races that the Yatavra controls. That is what Mocowas secretly fears. Soon, he will ask me to help him overwhelm the renegade forces who have joined up with even more pirates and scavengers from countless systems. Perhaps certain races will join them as well."

Valeskin stands up and places his hands behind his back. "The problem is the Reduzen queen building countless hunter cruisers somewhere and becoming stronger. She has taken a lot of territory on Trebaj that we will never get back, and her star ranger fighter patrols are to be feared. Soon she will plan a strike to cripple us permanently."

"Mocowas will slow her plan," Grandres said. "We must conquer the Lutresas war breeders first. Do not worry, my son. The System Lords want Xunaseta to suffer. Otherwise, I would have been ordered to stop my plans. And the Reduzen queen will never come above us. Her race will kneel before me with the Titan Crown upon my head. This is my destiny and must happen before my time on this planet ends, for I am the brute of Bretasi and will reign over all of my enemies in the end."

Chapter Nine

Mocowas approached Grand Lord Mistress Esekal, a female Yatavra strategist who had been one of his most ardent supporters. Mocowas walked into his private quarters from the observation deck connected to the room where he and Esekal, his closest ally within the ranks of the System Lords, had planned to wipe out the renegade forces and all who sided with them.

Esekal sat down in a high chair next to a holographic map of the galaxy they were in. She looked behind her into the observation deck and saw some stars in space, and she wondered if her ruthless streak would see her through the next few cycles of her life. Mocowas would die one day, and Hetkarej and the other System Lords all craved the power he had obtained by being one of the smartest System Lords ever. Esekal was Mocowas's pick, but she always had to keep an eye on dangerous peers.

Mocowas turned and followed Esekal's eyes. "We have many beings that we must punish before we begin to see a time where no race will think of challenging us in space or on any planet that we have power over. Even the Borshux miners secretly plotted and schemed. We rely on them too much, and now we must be wary of their leaders."

"I am more concerned with the Wesja traders," Esekal said. "We need them to control the universal credit system."

Mocowas sneered. "The traders created Zelcres credits, but they fear losing the support of the Giyehe and many other races. I have warned the head trader, Sadriki, that his mega city in space, Ultorious Prime, will always be under my protection. We follow his guidance in all things financially, but he must never go against us. He and I must be as one. Sadriki is smart, and I think he will remain loyal."

Esekal cracked a smile, which was rare. "I believe we can trust him, but I will arrange a meeting with representatives of the races that speak to him behind closed doors. There are some that he trusts more than others, and once we get them onside, we will be in a better position with the traders. After the wars have ended, there will be rewards for all who support us. That is what the message will be."

Mocowas sat in a wide high chair and played with a large purple diamond ring on his finger with a black and silver band.

"Give them enough credits to build new ships and ensure they get a percentage of some of the largest mines we have within seven planetary systems," he said. "Sometimes gifts work better than intimidation on those who must be swayed."

"You are right as usual, Mocowas. I will arrange it."

Mocowas stood up. He looked restless and tired, but he knew that there was much work to do.

"Follow me onto the bridge, Esekal," he said.

Once the automatic double doors opened, the two System Lords walked through the doorway before them. A loud, sharp, piercing sound like a whale song underwater aired out, then stopped just as the crew stood to attention.

Mocowas looked over the crew on the bridge, nodded, and looked out of the view screen. Fear of failure, which he sometimes felt, entered his body, took control of him for an instant, and quickly passed. He knew he was already at war even though Relentless's newly upgraded flagship had not yet fired a single shot in any space battle as one of the most protected space vessels in any Yatavra fleet. He travelled with eight hundred and fifty cruisers and five hundred carriers. He had one thousand close combat scout vessels at his disposal. Hundreds of carriers and cruisers could reach him within minutes using hyper-light speed as they were nearby. The renegade forces would struggle to bring the fight to the Supreme System Lord. He had made sure of this.

Mocowas was on his way to witness his first major battle. The renegade forces were secretly meeting with some space raiders who had recently decided to fight alongside them.

This would be the perfect time to test the fleet that had just been built, and Mocowas looked forward to seeing if his pilots and ship crews had what it took to defeat the enemy. Seven hundred cruisers and carriers had been sent to different regions of space to surround the renegades and the raiders. Relentless, the rest of the fleet had an overwhelming number of people to crush any enemy that opposed them. Mocowas's fleet commander, Grand Lord Master Pakowe, suspected that many hundred ships of different sizes would be at the meeting to hail the leaders of the future force to be reckoned with and celebrate the combined powers which would create a new renegade force that would bring about a crucial rebellion. But Mocowas saw them as looters, murderers, and maniacs. A lesser breed of scum who had no right to exist in the same universe as him.

Esekal stood next to Mocowas. "Soon, we will witness something special. I can feel it," she said. "Our power cannot be contained. We will prove that we are unstoppable."

Mocowas had pain in his back, which caused him discomfort. He sat in his chair and sighed.

"We will see whether our enemy makes errors in judgement or not," he said. "In the end, war is war, and foes die or survive. Whether they choose to fight or not, if they live, is up to them, but we must not lose our composure, Esekal. Soon, we will be able to focus on making sure that our allies do not become their own worst enemy. They are greedy, and I am sure many will challenge us. We must make an example of a powerful foe to show kings, queens, and emperors alike that we fear nobody who feels it is in their best interests to oppose us."

"I have devised a strategy that the Giyehe will never see coming, Mocowas. Though I fear the war we will embark on will be long and brutal, the Reduzen queen will feel threatened by our actions, which may make her rebel. But we will have to wait until the right moment to strike."

Mocowas almost growled as he responded. "Hetkarej will control Fasjey; I have told him I do not expect him to fail me now. He is supposed to be the best of all the System Lords beneath you, according to Gorxab, that fool who treats certain lords below him as if they are his siblings."

"Hetkarej is favoured by many and watched cautiously by few," Esekal said. "In our circle, there is not a soul who trusts him, but our circle is small."

Mocowas almost growled before answering, "I recognise this, but I have all the power, and those in league with me ultimately decide who gets the largest share of any wealth handed out to others. Hetkarej will move to the beat of my drum until I am gone. Then you must decide how he should use his powers as a System Lord once I am gone."

"We have no proof that Hetkarej is behaving in an underhand fashion, so he cannot be stripped of his powers as he is far too useful, but I wish it could be done," Esekal said. "For now, our enemies are his enemies, and he has proven to be loyal, but I sense he focuses too much on his agendas with the power we gave him. He questions the authority of the veteran System Lords who support you. He craves the power of the Kalicos kings, who were the Titans of their era. He wants to wear that crown he keeps on his ship. We must always know his movements and watch Grandres and his son Valeskin closely."

"Do not worry, Esekal. King Grandres needs wealth and land. You already had the miners offer him both. He will use many ships to protect the planets they will give him. He will be so worried about his vessels being attacked by Queen Fasjey's Reduzen hunter cruisers that he will order his fleet commander to use his galaxy cruiser fleets to regulate all the regions of space where the dark queen could challenge his power. We control them like pawns on the land we gave them whilst we never use our ships to stop their endless battle in space."

"The plan is working well, Supreme Lord," Esekal said.

Mocowas leaned forward on his view screen and saw several fleets approaching Relentless. It was Grand Lord Master Pakowe, who was also Mocowas's fleet commander, arriving with more ships. The vessels he came with had gold Cetilsun vertical metal strips all over them, with huge cannons lined up all over the ship's structure from top to bottom.

Missile platforms shaped like the wings of an eagle that looked vast in size were across the front of ships. The rectangular main body of the ship was beneath the wing-shaped front, and the bridge was on top and square-shaped. The ships were not pretty to look at. Still, they were designed to be defensive vessels capable of mass destruction in a space battle.

Pakowe's face appeared on the view screen. "Supreme Lord Mocowas. I am here to join the fleet. I have been waiting for the renegade fleet to get decimated for the longest time. Undoubtedly, I believe we will have to fight in the end. I am always ready to use every weapon when a battle is to be fought. Isn't that right, Esekal?"

Eseksl smiled and bowed slightly, "It is true you are one of the best at what you do, Pakowe."

Mocowas stood up. "Come, let us go to our chosen destination and meet the fleet. Pakowe, join us on Relentless before we go into hyperlight drive speed. We will speak about the trial we face. The true test will begin once the rest of the renegade learn of the attack."

"The pirate who gave us the coordinates to the rendezvous point has disappeared, as I suspected," Esekal said. "No matter, he was useful while the relationship lasted."

Pakowe sniggered. "None of these pirates can be trusted. I will be with you soon.
I look forward to speaking with you some more, Supreme Lord."

The view screen showed Pakowe's fleet again, and Mocowas turned and walked to his private quarters with Esekal close behind him. He was certain of victory, but he feared more than half the ships he had with him were in jeopardy, even with the element of surprise on their side. The renegade force had been challenging to fight; some were genius captains and commanders. He needed to think and speak of the future of his race. Building his empire concerned him more than anything else. As far as he was concerned, winning all the wars coming his way would seal his name in history and make his legacy great. The defeat of his enemy was something he desired more than anything else that was on his mind.

Chapter Ten

Ikizuni walked down the gangway of the flagship Ravage, a ship he had captained for so long, and he felt sad. The legendary ship was embarking on a new voyage. The renegade force needed to find a new planet to settle where they could not be found. A base was required to plan a series of attacks to slow down the enemy and make them realise that the renegades were true warriors.

The brave captain of his ship was a veteran of combat in space. There had been talk of making him the fleet commander for the entire renegade force. He was known to be deadly under pressure, as much as he proved to be a leader who got results when it counted. Nothing could stop him from attacking when he was angry in the past. However, he had committed to controlling his temperament over the last few cycles because he believed that made him a more effective captain, which was better for his crew. All those who followed him loved him and would die for him instantly. This made Ikizuni feel like the world would be in the palm of his hands once his troubles were over. However, Mocowas was a foe with the resources to defeat more than one emperor at once. While the renegade force was mighty, with countless battle warriors, including ingenious pilots in many systems, ready to fight in any number of battles, winning a war would take more than one or two cycles.

Ikizuni walked onto a diagonal gangway that connected to an observation deck, which had an adjoining war room filled with holographic maps of planets, star charts, and a small library of critical history books filled with facts and information about different species, including their environments and habits. Some engineers were in the observation room, tinkering with devices, including wrist communicators and some of the sensors in the rooms that project holograms. Ikizuni waited in the war room, and as he did, the engineers finished their work and left him in peace. Captain Redejanto of the Noxret race walked into the observation room. Like many in his race, he was one of the stealthiest humanoids on board. Though he was shorter than most of the beings around at 5'9", he moved fast and struck hard with a soul blade. This was a popular weapon amongst his kind, with the blade the Noxret used being curved with a laser on its surface edge that burnt the skin as it cut deep. The Noxret captain had a thick, chunky head atop a lanky, worn-looking body. This is why his race was so deceptive, and those who never knew of the reputation of the cunning Noxret wild warriors, who were the best fighters, would eventually be overpowered or outsmarted. As Redejanto's eyes, which looked too small for his bulgy head, darted from left to right, he closed his blazer and clicked the bones in his long fingers with sharp nails. He then grinned at Ikizuni, showing his wide teeth. The captain stopped himself from fidgeting and scratched the skin on his neck, which was blue with a shade of purple running through the middle of his skin in the area up his face to his forehead.

Redejanto looked out of the view screen to see the stars in the kosotrox system. It was filled with wasteland planets, which had been popular haunts for scavengers in the past who dwelled on the land that was barren and dead. They survived only to suffer ions ago. This was not somewhere his renegade force could stay. There was hope of a meeting with those who described themselves as Scavenger Lords. Still, they had hidden themselves away, and they were the kind of warriors who would find those they wanted to fight with when they felt the need to prove themselves. Ikizuni thought they were talking about how the brothers and sisters they once fought with were in a war that would never be forgotten.

Redejanto spoke in a husky, broken voice, "I believe our numbers are about to double. The pirates that have been with us for many cycles have told me that the Pirate Lords who hid themselves for so long have decided to join us. The old Scavenger Lords will surely follow. Long ago, they fought against the Pirate Lords. Still, they fought a common enemy, Emperor Zarodavak, side by side a few cycles later when he tried to destroy them all after the death of his brother at the hands of Pirate Lord Lurazani and the Scavenger Lord Ukerijal. Now, we must fight as one."

"I pray you get your wish, but I will not count on the Scavenger Lords' support. They are still reeling from the defeat they suffered at the hands of the warlords they battled with before I became a veteran pilot. They lost more souls than any of our minds could see."

"Ikizuni, you speak the truth that has been seen and written by all, but revenge is sweet, and the Yatavra-System Lords that ruled during the era we speak of plotted and schemed with the warlords they controlled to see the Scavenger Lords meet their ugly fate," Redejanto said in a grave voice. The System Lords have also plotted with the warlords to kill all the pirates if possible, so we have more than one thing in common with the scavengers. Ikizuni looked at the star maps to the left of him, and he could see the destination the ship was heading for. He then allowed himself to gaze as he studied the patterns of the stars on the map.

"I have often wondered what our universe would be like if blood had not been shed and there was only peace," he said. "I feel depressed when I see how much we have lost."

"Do not feel sorrow, Ikizuni. We will free all the alien breeds that we protect."

"I hope that is true because if we fail, it will only make Mocowas even more powerful, and he will make others suffer under his incredibly evil reign. His wrath is as cold and dark as Grandres. Still, he has more power, and I feel he may have an even greater hunger when conquering kingdoms in other galaxies far from here."

"That monster is the fire demon that spreads fear throughout many lands. Any being cannot stop his form of hatred. He feels no love for another, I am sure, and he never protected a young member of his race like he was his loving son or gentle daughter."

"Redejanto, you do not have to tell me about the heartless brute who only sees the game of the master and treats every being as if they are the wanted prey. Mocowas will feel the crooked blade from an enemy one day, and then his System Lords will scurry like frightened sea worms."

Captain Asutex walked into the observation room. He walked strong, and people called him the Rotumze destroyer when he was a boy. He knocked down every problem with his tall, 6'4", wide, heavy-set, half-masculine, half-stiff fat frame. Every step the dark brown, strong-boned, sharp-eyed killer took was a large one that covered a lot of ground and made a being feel unsafe walking in front of him. He was a hulk of a captain, exuded confidence, and respected those who used any prowess they possessed as he did.

"I have news from the renegades who have been patrolling space sectors in the Trejorgas system near the Wesja trader's planet Ultorious Prime, where we have been fighting the Borshux attackers," he said. "Mewetesi has been sending fighters to patrol space long distances from where he truly is to make others believe he is capable of being everywhere and anywhere as far as they are concerned. Soon, it may be that the Lutresas race will be our main allies. If Queen Fasjey and her Reduzen beast warriors join us along with the Giyehe, my friends, we would be a force to be reckoned with. Mocowas would truly fear us, too, but we must never hesitate and always be ready to fight, drawing first blood at every possible moment. Mocowas would truly fear us then."

Ikizuni laughed. "Asutex, I have never seen you so excited for as long as I have been your friend. Calm yourself. There is very little confirmation in the message you sent us. All I see are the dreams of rebellious minds that I admit we need, but we must stay grounded. As leaders, we need to focus. I don't need my pilots starting rumours that bear no truth."

"Asutex nearly growled. "Why do we have all these ground troops hidden on barren lands, Ikizuni? They wait and wait, but they never get to fight."

"Think of what your great spirit walkers would say, Asutex, Ikizuni said. "We must build weapons and protect our bases on cold moons that were left by sinners who suffered on dark lands with heartless terrain in regions where our foe would never think to look for us. Our duty is to ensure the troops are ready to fight the enemy with honour and valour. Soon, our time will come, but patience is useful to the warrior willing to wait for the right moment to strike."

"All who know of the name Asutex have always spoken of the one whose spirits tell him when to fight with every fibre of his being, with his supporters behind him, and we must attack all the ports that we can with everything we have now."

Redejanto laughed. "One day, you will speak of the glory days like the legend you are, Asutex, and nobody will ever forget how you told the stories about the battles we won. But we will attack in stages, learn more about our enemies' responses and predict their counterattacks to the point where they hesitate and make mistakes. Then, we will truly make them suffer. I will see the Yatavra-System Lords die in flames until the war is over, and then we will rip down that which they have built to tear simple, harmless beings down. I will ensure this happens even if the fight continues for as long as I live."

Ikizuni looked at the star maps again, and then a crew member walked into the room. It was a male communications officer.

"Sir, we have a message from one of our new moon bases," he said. "It is General Tucawaz of the Hecazy ground forces."

Ikizuni looked concerned and wanted to look directly at Asutux, whom he knew to be somebody who could get support from critical members of the renegade force who, like him, do not like to be opposed.

Ikizuni walked past the communications officer. "All of you come. Let us see what the general wants."

As the forward-thinking captain of the ship walked with his peers behind him, he tried to put himself in Asutux's position. He had suffered more than anybody there. The original Rotumze spirit walkers among his people had almost been wiped out, and the System Lords had wanted this for ions. They hated the clan of visionaries who helped to define more than one era shaped by a unique culture filled with legendary characters whom the gods blessed according to more than one group of philosophers and even conquerors who had lost wars to the skilled fighters. Ikizuni felt his friend's pain, but he had to be sure that the renegade force would send many blows in the direction of the enemy over a long period. He could not afford to waste resources or let a single warrior die because of an ill-fated plan made too hastily.

Ikizuni entered the war room near the secondary bridge with the other renegade captains. A holograph appeared when he and his brothers-in-arms stood before the communication systems. A ghostly-looking dark blue humanoid with a bony face, dressed in a black overall-looking bodysuit with metallic armour and a short orange blazer, stood firm, looking like a hard day's work had worn him away. This is how the Hecazy race looked more often than not. At one point, Ikizuni regularly joked that it was hard to tell when a military man was lazy or not when you were in the company of the Hecazy army and their much-talked-about space force battle pilots. But he stopped making those jokes when he learned of how they worked once their numbers dwindled after they were attacked by several warlord factions trying to start their own federation like the warlord Souls galactic force once the Takrezac warlords broke up. A bioweapon was used that killed many beings in their home world, Vaskalta, over one cycle. Then, many were made to starve in their home world by the Yatavra- System Lords for another three cycles as they feared the Hecazy warriors who fought with their allies to stop the union of the warlords fighting a war where more atrocities were committed by all who were involved over a short period than during any other war in the new age. The Hecazy became paranoid when it came to outsiders, and the System Lords found a reason to hate a race they could not control.

Tucuwaz, a Hecazy battleaxe, moved closer to the screen on his end. "How are you, future Commander? Even though I am hidden far away, I hear the rumours all beings speak of. And why am I so hidden? Why have we not stormed the gates of our enemy's allies as part of a pre-emptive strike to stop Mocowas from adding to his ever-growing numbers? We have millions of troops over many systems, waiting to attack. Races who have been betrayed and spat upon for what seems like an eternity want to decimate cities and ruin our foe. All it takes is a word to start the attack. I ask you, Ikizuni. Have we picked the right leaders for the battles we must fight?"

In his younger days, Ikizuni would've felt threatened by this, but he was now experienced. "I must think about the impact any battles will have on our numbers and whether we have an advantage by attacking a target or are we simply showing that we can use brute force to kill to prove a point. If this does not dent the System Lords' armour, we have proven nothing. Mistakes can teach lessons and cause pitfalls that lead to one's demise. We can't afford to make them, and if we do, how many brave military experts, fine veteran soldiers, and young-born fighters do you think we will lose?"

"I see you have thought about your answer, Ikizuni," Tucuwaz said. "I can tell you that I have never been so confident that we can win this war. We have the upper hand, as Mocowas will not know how many have joined our cause. He still thinks we are just a force made up of a few outsiders who are not under the command of more powerful renegades. Even though the races who have joined us need more advanced weaponry for their ground forces, their ships can more than match the System Lords' older ships. The allies of the races we have called to fight with us could give us endless resources and help us to liberate those who suffer, helping lost souls to find shelter and grow so they can become strong and vibrant."

Asutux speaks cautiously, "I have plans for many ground troops, so I need them to be prepared. How many scavenger engineers are you using to build weaponry, and where are they getting their parts from?"

Tucuwaz replied, "You already know that the scavengers have contacts in countless systems. Do not forget that there is more than one warlord who would love to be free from the grasp of the System Lords. Not all of them crave Mocowas's attention. It is they who would like to set the standard over time. My friends, the warlords will become a danger on an intergalactic scale once more once the System Lords have been defeated like they were so long ago."

Ikizuni's mood changed, and his face became dark. "Tucuwaz, the times ahead will be the hardest we have ever faced. It seems there will always be a war to be won. If that is what the future holds for us, then so be it. Our soldiers will be ready to face the painful reality just like we have been for so many cycles. Let us not frown on this, for tragedy is not the only thing we will see. There will be times we rejoice as we take territories and claim victories after blood has been spilt from open wounds. We must remember that we are responsible for protecting our followers with our lives so they may live to tell their own stories and build a life for themselves in a haven where justice exists. The righteous can benefit from this for many cycles to come. I have promised our warriors and their families that we will achieve this, and I keep my promises, for that is how I have always been."

Chapter Eleven

Heturadi stood on the bridge of a gargantuan cube-shaped galaxy cruiser that approached Lutresas's home world in the Torechen system. He walked forward and stood next to the ship's pilot, a gruesome-looking small Kalicos male with slight swelling under his tired eyes, a podgy face, and small spots on his forehead.

Heturadi gave an order to the pilot. "Take us out of hyper-light speed as soon as we pass the ends of the space sector where the Netarta nebula can be seen."

The pilot responded, "Yes, commander."

Heturadi put his hands on the pilot's shoulder. "It has been a long time since I saw the purple, red, and turquoise-looking clouds of the Netarta nebula. Before we can glance upon it from afar, we will be met by the fierce Lutresas vessels that may patrol the area. But we have a task to complete. The destruction of an enemy that is bred to fight. Thousands of gladiators will die when we attempt to overrun the queen of the war breeder's cities so that we can destroy the seven palaces that represent the spirits of the princes and princesses who were lost in the war between the Lutresas warmongers and the last of the Otrizon clone barons a few cycles ago. Picking the right side was never something Queen Xunaseta was good at. Now she will suffer a cruel fate because she fights alongside the Reduzen queen."

The pilot looked straight ahead and never moved but spoke, "I will make sure I tell you when

I take the ship out of hyperlight drive speed, Commander Heturadi."

"Make sure that you do, pilot," Heturadi said.

Heturadi took his hand off the pilot's shoulder, walked up to his chair, and sat down.

As the all-conquering fleet commander looked ahead at the view screen, he thought about his advantages in numbers when it came to space vessels. Then he wondered how much support Queen Fasjey would give her allies.

Heturadi addressed the crew on the bridge. "This is my ship. I gave my ship no name, but she is an avenger when necessary and will take no prisoners when she attacks. War is my craft, and death lurks within my mind and causes me to feel that my blood should be as black as my heart. Bring me victory, Siritusu, God of conquerors, and I shall ensure the feast I have in your honour will be great."

The pilot spoke in a clear, raised voice, "We are about to come out of hyper-light drive speed now, Commander Heturadi."

"Good, scan the area as soon as possible," Heturadi said. "I want no surprises."

"Yes, Commander," the pilot said.

The pilot scanned for enemy vessels when the ship came out of hyperlight drive speed. The ship's size and shape made it look monstrous. Cannons were lined up on either side of the vessel in rows going downwards. There were several rows on top of the vessels. The cannons were all different shapes and sizes. Cannons on rotating turrets were at the lower front of the ship. Missile platforms were also at the front of the ship, above and below the bridge deck at the front of the structure and halfway down from the top of the vessel. Many fleets of cube-shaped boats of different sizes were rectangular in the area where the attackers were held. In the middle, where the security decks and gladiators were, was a large domestic area built like a small city within the vessels. These ships were also incredible in size. They looked like powerful structures with genius architecture that could withstand time. Heturadi had brought five thousand with him.

The pilot turned and looked at his Commander. "Sir, there are no ships near us except our own."

Heturadi spoke with a severe voice, "For now. Soon, the war breeder's patrols will spot the second smaller fleet sent to attack the other Lutresas planets. I am sure they are close to their target. It will not be long before the enemy sends out patrols, and we are attacked by many. I will speak with General Vatemfa in his quarters about our strategies for the attack. Alert me at the first sign of any danger."

"Yes, sir," the pilot said.

Heturadi walked off the bridge and down a long diagonal gangway linked to the shuttle shafts. He got into a shuttle that was larger than the kind that is on most ships that had ever been built. Only the Yatavra had shafts as big as the Kalicos ships on their storage vessels. This was one of the reasons the feared fleet commander believed he could one day challenge the Yatavra fleet and beat their forces in an awesome space battle that would undoubtedly happen in the future.

Heturadi loudly said, "Take me to level ten senior officer's deck A."

The doors closed, and the shuttle travelled down the shaft at an incredible speed. The shuttle stopped, and the doors opened. Heturadi stepped off the shuttle and walked down a gangway slightly slanted downwards. The gangway straightened up as Heturadi passed several large quarters. He then reached two massive private quarters that were side by side. One was Vatemfa's study, and the other was his living quarters. Heturadi pressed a touchscreen on a panel next to the door with a speaker attached, which beeped three times and alerted Vatemfa that he had arrived.

Vatemfa answered, "Who is it?"

The fleet commander replied, "It is Heturadi."

"Come in, my friend," the general said.

The double doors opened, and Heturadi entered the room to see Vatemfa finishing a large bowl of fish stew. He put the silver spoon he held in the golden bowl and patted his chest hard as he swallowed.

"The flesh on the head of the sakreva fish is always hard to swallow, but I enjoy it, old friend."

Heturadi smiled. "I know you are always ready to talk about war after a good meal, Vatemfa, so here I am. I have gone over the plans, and we will see this thing through till the end, but I feel that many will be scarred for life when we come up against the war breeders' slayers."

Vatemfa wiped his mouth with a small cloth and spoke, "Grandres feels the same way, but we must do what must be done. This fight has been coming for a long time. Fighting the Lutresas killing machines was always going to happen. It is happening sooner than I originally thought, making no difference."

"Have you spoken with the top gladiators you command?"

"Heturadi, you know they need no words of encouragement from me. The gladiators remember everything they had been taught each time they went to war. They know that winning is everything."

"You were always there for them when they were young and in training, Vatemfa. You have done that, and they respect you for it."

"I demand that of myself, and they always prove loyal and ready to die," the general said proudly.

Heturadi paced back and forth. "Will the blood legions lead the attack, or will you use a different tactic?"

Vatemfa answered, "The blood legions will be part of the second wave. This will be a tough invasion. Suppose we do not lose half of the gladiators due to the Lutresas fleet attacking our carriers before we get near the planet. In that case, we have a good chance of winning the battle on land."

"After the Lutresas have seen the fleet approaching, they will prepare for battle on a large scale," Heturadi said. "The fleet that will attack the planets where the enemy harvests much of their food and supplies for the cold winters. We shall see if the war breeders' legends have what it takes to survive another great war. They beat the clone barons but lost many heroes and legends, some of whom were superior thinkers regarding battle tactics. This was a great blow for them. We will kill off their military and see the cities they had the genius Cetilsun architects of old build for them turned to rubble and dust. The Cetilsun race has always favoured the Lutresas race. They love their flamboyance and the way that they flaunt their wealth. Soon, no more business will come to them from Queen Xunaseta."

Vatemfa grunted. "They call her the queen of the slayers. Her last strike against the clone baron planets, after the young members of the royal bloodline's palaces on different planets were attacked, was so devastating that the war was deemed a stalemate, and a truce was quickly made. Now, the last barons have become recluses as they rebuild their empire. Only certain architects have been allowed near the three planetary systems they now control. I have heard that the factory cities are a sight to behold. But that is just a rumour for now. It was a nasty war over territory and for pride's sake."

"Now Queen Fasjey's fleets patrol the two planetary systems Xunaseta took from the barons."

"Heturadi, you have already told me that a fleet of hunter cruisers has been sent to the Lutresas queen," Vatemfa said as he became angrier by the second. "The Giyehe have been hard at work building new cruisers for Queen Fasjey, and Mocowas knows it. He wants this war to happen and thinks he conceals it well. The Yatavra is using us; they control us simply because they can."

Heturadi's temper mirrored Vatemfa's: "Over one hundred and fifty thousand new ships were launched from space stations and space patrol bases just a few days ago, and the Yatavra plan to launch triple the amount twenty days from now from newly built shipyards in thirty-six different systems. No one race can equal the System Lords' power. Their accumulated wealth is unbelievable, and their ability to crush the enemy is worrying. A combined force of races can beat them, but they are fully aware of the danger surrounding their kind."

Vatemfa growls, then speaks with his fist clenched, "Mocowas is only concerned with his legacy. His existence makes my brain burn and my blood boil like the desert heat from planet Pesdrokar." The general began to sweat as his body temperature rose from his stress. He turned to see his pet kiwoyiz lizard from the planet he had just referred to. It was lounging in the corner of the room. The lizard is red with a long body, including a hard-skinned tail. Its eyes were blue and oval-shaped, and it was continuously looking from left to right.

Heturadi shouted, "I hate that Mocowas has not questioned Fasjey about these new cruisers! Yesterday, there were reports that Reduzen cruisers and carriers were sent to space regions to protect certain territories, and the Giyehe engineers-built ships for that treacherous queen. A clear sign of a union that will cause a major intergalactic problem for us in the future!"

Vatemfa seethed. "Mocowas will not blink an eyelid unless it directly threatens the Yatavra race's existence. I am a general who knows it. The fool sees these things the Reduzen queen is doing as simple efforts to antagonise Grandres."

"You are right. Mocowas is a fool, and every member of the Kalicos royal court knows it."

"Let us look at the facts, Heturadi. The Borshux miners have held secret talks with us about whose side they will take if a full-scale intergalactic war between many nations and the Yatavra-System Lords breaks out and Mocowas forces start to lose. They will support us, and so will Emperor Oltexav Sequay, the leader of the Derusav race. Their homeworld, Esyoret, is one of the largest planets on record. They have a military that once scared Mocowas for many cycles as they fought over planetary systems and regions of space until he felt that he equalled the power of Oltexav as a so-called supreme being and quickly called for a truce to be made before he lost too much territory. There are other planets close to the size of Esyoret that Oltexav controls, including planets where he has mines filled with different coloured diamonds and planets with gem canyons that dwarf our own with food stocks that will last forever. Other emperors will follow his lead. He has told the miners this and is due to meet Grandres at the end of this cycle after the harvest festival. We will be a mighty force when the long war comes; believe me, it will be the longest war, and we will be great commanders who see suffering and death. But we will be victorious."

Heturadi pondered as he tried to find a place in his mind where there was no chaos and darkness in his race's future unless they fought perhaps more than one major war that would mean countless lives were lost. Darkness would grace their doorstep for at least a while. He knew the next few cycles would be filled with death and destruction. It was an outcome that he was used to seeing as those born to conquerors must accept that the darkest fate can become the truest reality for any commander.

"The problem we will face is that the Reduzen queen can fend for herself in a storm filled with horrification and mayhem. Fasjey will try to kill everything in sight with the Giyehe as allies and all the other races who support them," he said. "They will never have to bow to a single living soul if they win. So, to stop them from overpowering us, we will try to use our military power to regulate many systems near them. You already know this as a general, and I think my job will be difficult because of the new Reduzen cruisers."

Heturadi's wrist comm badge made a lengthy beep. Then the ship's pilot spoke, "Commander, we have been spotted by several massive fleets of Reduzen cruisers and Lutresas carriers escorted by Star Ranger fighters. Hundreds of these ships are coming towards us at high impulse speeds."

Heturadi ordered, "Alert the fleet commanders to create a defensive line of five hundred carriers and three hundred and twenty cruisers to be ready to engage. Send a message to the rest of the fleet's captains to hold their position unless I send for them. The size and strength of our ships cannot be matched. We do not need heavy numbers to outdo our foe before we reach the planet where we will meet the bulk of the Lutresas main fleet and the Reduzen ships that support them."

"Yes, sir," the pilot said.

Heturadi turned around and started to walk slowly towards the doors. "Vatemfa, you will want to see how this plays out. Those carriers will be transporting fighters to other regions of space to bulk up the enemy's defences. This will be our first true test."

Vatemfa stood up, caught up with Heturadi, and walked out of the private quarters together. As they approached the shuttle shaft, Heturadi wondered how the second fleet would fare once they engaged the enemy. Once they split up, space stations would be attacked. Then, when they were close to the Lutresas planets, where their most valuable mines were, they would regroup and aim to control the mining planets. Eight more fleets were waiting in the Vetracasi system to take gladiators to three of the planets the Lutresas used for entertainment. Millions of citizens were in each of the cities on these planets, and they were prey that must be captured. The defences were solid but would be no match for the massive fleets that were sent to deal with them as far as Heturadi was concerned. However, he was aware the Lutresas war breeders who built the military were no fools, and they protected their kind well. The Reduzen were on call to give their allies all the needed assistance. Grandres wanted to control the planetary systems that the clone barons once owned. A fleet had been sent to these systems as well. There was a strong chance that Ujesal, the Reduzen fleet commander, would have large numbers in these systems. Still, Heturadi had prepared his captains for every kind of outcome. They had a massive number of ships at their disposal.

Both Kalico's superiors got onto the shuttle, and the doors opened when they reached the end of the gangway.

Heturadi turned to the comm system on the shuttle and said, "Bridge." His voice sounded deeper than usual. He was in fighting mode and could only think about ensuring the right tactics were used in this battle.

The shuttle stopped on the bridge deck on level ten. Heturadi and Vatemfa got off the shuttle and walked down the short gangway onto the bridge to see some cruisers changing their formation so that they were in a defensive position that would protect Heturadi's ship. Other cruisers and carriers lined up in a row on either side in an attack formation, with some being positioned diagonally. The Kalicos carriers had the same basic design as the Galaxy cruisers. Still, the living quarters were larger as some intergalactic gladiators and added ship security were on board. As a rule, whenever Vatemfa travelled with the fleets, the gladiators were stationed on the carriers. The carriers in the first line of defence broke off into five groups. Then they surged forward at impulse speeds, stopping in front of the ship they were protecting with a barricade. The ships waited to meet the Reduzen and Lutresas fighters approaching with primed cannons.

The carriers in front and seventy-five of the Kalicos carriers that were further behind Heturadi's ship opened their bay doors, and hundreds of close combat vessels poured out into the dark depths of space. The grey and crimson-coloured attackers flew ahead to meet the enemy fighters before they got to the fleet. The attacker's pilots wanted to create a space graveyard with their enemy's bodies. The vessels looked frightening as they surged forward together and met the Lutresas fighters further in the distance, which could barely be seen in the main bridge's view screen without magnification technology being used.

Heturadi looked at the bridge communications operator and said, "Give the order to the pilots in the attackers. Tell them to focus on the Star Ranger fighters. Then order fifty-five of the Kalicos carriers behind us to be ready to release their attackers in case we need to replenish the line of close combat vessels."

The carriers behind Heturadi's ship backed up and spread out. The pilots of every attacker knew they were lying in wait, ready to face a large assault from violent predators. There was no escaping their fate, even if they were not part of the first wave.

Heturadi stood by his chair and remained silent for a moment. "Steady. We will wait for the light flashes in the dark to be close to the ships till we send the second wave of attackers."

Just as Heturadi finished talking, large orange and white flashes could be seen in the distance. The flashes moved closer and closer at a slow pace. These were explosions in space, and Heturadi fumed as he knew his pilots were being killed in battle. All of the green and blue laser fire of the enemy and the red laser fire of the Kalicos attackers could be seen by all, and the vessels were getting closer and closer.

Heturadi knew he needed to be alert and immediately ensure the attackers joined the fight. He was known for his patience and determination. People told stories about it on Daheza.

Heturadi and Vatemfa knew that Grandres had ordered millions of Kalicos citizens to be resettled on new worlds that the miners would provide. He was expanding his empire, and he knew Mocowas was too distracted by the war with the renegades to attempt to put the fear of the gods into him as a warning not to get above himself. If Heturadi managed to invade Lutresas, that would weaken the Reduzen queen. Grandres would have more than a clear advantage even though the queen still had the Giyehe race and many who supported them as her allies.

The ships got closer, and then many explosions started to occur. The Reduzen cruisers were doing their worst. The hunter cruisers were bulky in areas most shielded by green Cetilsun metal plating, but they were still long and sleek in their own way. The nose of the ships was especially long. Laser cannons on turrets are on the top, bottom, and side of the nose of the ship, and the slightly long wings of the ship have laser cannons underneath. There are missile platforms lined up along the top of the ship. The hunter cruisers had a massive bridge. The new fleets were mighty. They had destroyed countless Kalicos attackers, but Heturadi's fleet had carriers transporting more fighters than the Lutresas carriers. He was convinced he would see off the threat that was coming effectively enough.

Heturadi waited for an instant when he saw the Reduzen Star Ranger fighters that had managed to make it through the first wave of Kalicos attackers flying through the flames and debris left by the Kalicos attackers. He took a few deep breaths. Heturadi knew what must come next.

"Tell the pilots to engage now," he said. "Let's see these Reduzen worms squirm up close."

The attackers flew forward. The communications operator and his assistant could hear the Kalicos pilots screaming and swearing out loud, and they fired their lasers. Their cube-shaped ships with a pointed end where the pilot was situated were deceptively fast. The Kalicos only picked pilots with the best training records to fly close combat vessels.

The Reduzen Star Ranger fighters were half-cylinder-looking vessels with slightly jagged, rigid circular noses that looked like they had sharp eyes carved into the metallic structure. The ship's rear was the shape of a half-moon with the propulsion system underneath it. This was a unique stern, and it was well-shielded. They were no faster than the Kalicos ships, but they manoeuvred better.

Once the vessels crossed each other, it was easy to see that the Star Ranger fighters were outnumbered and outmatched as they were blown away by precision shots from more than one Kalicos attacker at a time in many instances. There were two direct attacks where the pilots flew at each other and then circled to do the same thing again. The second time around, more Star Ranger fighters joined the lines and lines of fighters that sped up as they charged into one another in a head-on battle. Surprisingly, there was not one collision as the speeds at which pilots were flying were dangerously fast whilst firing their lasers. The front and sides of the Kalicos ships were hit, and the Star Ranger pilots' jagged noses of their ships were smashed and shattered as they burst into flames and crashed into other fighters close by.

A hectic dogfight ensued, and the Star Ranger pilots were eager to excel. Their strategic behaviour pattern had always been to draw attackers in, make the angles in a fight between two pilots as tight as possible, and take advantage. The fighters weaved in between other ships, dodging other battles as they took place. They kept their distance from the Kalicos galaxy cruisers and carriers that would soon use their laser cannons. The Kalicos were biding their time and playing with them. The Reduzen fighters couldn't aim for the cruisers while fighting the attackers; they were luring them into a tactical trap for another Star Ranger to take a shot. The cannons on the Kalico's behemoth-looking vessels were also hard to destroy. It took far more than one focused shot to damage them.

Countless fighters were exploding in a ball of light, and then Heturadi made his next move.

"Send a message to the carriers on standby to be ready to send in more of our attackers," he said. "We must be fully prepared for the Lutresas fighters to advance when it happens."

As the orders were relayed to the captains aboard the other ships, Heturadi sat down and considered whether he would have to use more ships for the battle he was watching. He quickly decided what his next move was.

Heturadi gave another order. "Tell captains on the cruisers and carriers that are in position to fire on every target they can."

"Yes, sir," the communications operator and his assistant said simultaneously.

The Kalicos attackers were picking off as many Star Ranger fighters as possible. Still, the Reduzen pilots were holding their ground. Then, suddenly, the cruiser captains got involved in the battle. The cannon operators started shooting their targets. The brown Reduzen hunter cruisers reacted by moving into an attack position, firing their laser cannons at every attacker in sight and firing on the Kalicos cruisers who returned fire. The Lutresas released their fighters from the carriers once they had flown into position. The newly built dark green and yellow fighters were long and low. They were roundish on the bottom half and slightly flat on the top half, with the vessel having a heavy cannon at the back of the top half of the vessel and one on either side of the ship. There were small flaps at the stern of the vessel. The back end was higher than the front, but the pilots practically leaned forward in the ships to fly them because of the design of the vessels. The ships were among the fastest in any galaxy known to the Kalicos, but they felt they had come prepared to fight them. These vessels were built to combat the new Kalicos attackers.

Heturadi turned his head and looked at the operator, "The captains of the new carriers must release our fighters now."

While the communications operator gave the order, Heturadi contemplated how bad the battle would truly be when they got closer to the planet. More ships were undoubtedly on the way, and the enemy fought well. The numbers and battle plan looked good, but things could go wrong. He was still confident of victory, but now it was clear that the losses would be greater. He looked at the floor and took a breath. His impression of the situation is that the task ahead was still by no means impossible, and he was still at an advantage due to the skill his captains had. The Lutresas had fought wars, but they were not born conquerors. The war breeders had met their match, as far as Heturadi was concerned.

The Lutresas attackers flew around the debris floating in the space's dark abyss. They aimed with the sharpest accuracy and were used to hunting solo. Despite their similar shape, the new Kalicos fighters were smaller than the old fighters. The cube was taller by a fraction, the ships were lighter, and the ships had shorter pointed ends. These ships were faster, and the cannons on the vessel's side were more powerful. The propulsion systems were safer and more reliable as they needed to be serviced less, and the ships were more durable.

As the attackers started to fire on the Lutresas fighters, the Reduzen began to hunt in packs. The Reduzen captains were concerned with the number of fighters Heturadi had at his disposal, but they were expecting this. More of the new Lutresas and Reduzen carriers were on their way. They could hold eighty-five Lutresas fighters and one hundred Star Ranger fighters used for long battles in outer space. The close combat vessels carried heavier laser cannons than usual, which packed a heavier punch than other ships of their size.

The Reduzen cruisers started firing on the Kalicos attackers, and the Star Rangers broke into smaller packs, fighting tooth and nail. The battle still felt like it had only just begun. Some pilots felt these were the last few seconds of their lives. But they knew everything happening around them and how much time had elapsed. If they were truly going to battle until the last ships were still in orbit unscathed by the dangerous battle that ensued, then this part of the battle could last a while.

As the smaller Kalicos attackers started to try to circle many of the Star Ranger fighter packs and fly between them to separate them, the Reduzen cruisers singled them out and fired their lasers. The Star Ranger pilots did their best to capitalise as they knew that the hunter cruisers' cannon operators would try to clear huge areas of space of the enemy attackers so they could work in sync with the fighter pilots and start to give them a clear path when it came to facing the following line of attackers from the carriers in Heturadi's fleet.

The Lutresas fleet had been training with the Reduzen fleet for over twenty cycles. The methods their allies were using were not new to them. The well-bred pilots were chasing down every possible kill with gritted teeth. The pilot's brown and white helmets had clear visors and a holographic date going down the side and top where their flat foreheads were. The Lutresas pilots were said to be bred to near perfection as far as the Yatavra was concerned. Their jealousy was why they never went out of their way to stop the war Grandres had planned with his advisors, who counselled him. Mocowas did not like the idea of Queen Fasjey having such a powerful ally. He would not tell Grandres that directly, but he would rather see the Lutresas race wiped out than see them survive any war. He was also dealing with the Otrizo clone barons and wanted to use them to create more cloned troops.

The Lutresas race-bred their warriors to think fast and move quicker. Many warriors had been called a work of art in their time because of their excellent fighting technique, and the best minds created them for their race. The Lutresas scientists who worked for the military ensured the warriors on the battlefield and the pilots for the space force were always masculine, with the same looking features, usually having quite a wide nose, a strong jawline, and a medium build. Many of the battlefield warriors were built to be taller than 6'7" with a wide frame and were made to be agile and virile. The best male specimens were used to breed with the strongest females, but genetics chambers were mostly used to create beings. Any child who was born with long-term illnesses had a slim chance of survival in a heartless society.

Heturadi leaned forward in his chair. Vatemfa had walked up to the view screen and stood to the left of his friend's chair.

"This will not be a clean victory, but we already knew that, Heturadi. Many will suffer and die once we get the gladiators to the Qukosi battlefield. The Lutresas warriors do not want to see the citizens on their planet suffer, so they will do their utmost to slay us all."

Heturadi did not respond to Vatemfa. "Be ready for more cruisers to arrive. The enemy will have called for reinforcements. Many will come."

The Reduzen cruisers lined up one after another. Other fleet commanders would've become anxious, but Heturadi did not, as his pilot pulled back. All forty cruisers he had ordered to separate themselves from the main fleet stayed in front of his ship and lined up in eight rows.

Heturadi called out, "Give the order to captains of sixty cruisers to move themselves into a defensive position around the carriers behind us. Tell another fifty cruisers to break in two and line up on either side of us at a further distance and await my orders. Make sure you tell them to give us as much room as possible. We have trained for this. I want no mistakes."

The Lutresas carriers released the last fighters to defend them from attack with the Star Ranger fighters as the cruisers fought each other. The Kalicos galaxy cruisers and carriers fired their lasers and missiles at the new Reduzen hunter cruisers built to look like the Star Ranger fighters but were far greater in size. They had a far stronger hull than their predecessor and various cannons, anti-gravity torpedoes, and missiles.

The Reduzen cruisers fired everything they had, and they never missed the target. The first missiles and torpedoes hit, but weaknesses in the large cubes were not exposed immediately. The newer Reduzen cruisers took on the maximum firepower that some older ships couldn't handle. There would never be a loss of life because one vessel tried to take blows to protect another, so those ships suffered huge losses in terms of the crew.

The hunter cruisers surged forward simultaneously at high impulse speeds, and then suddenly, the Star Ranger and Lutresas fighters attacked the Kalicos galaxy cruisers with them. The Kalicos cruisers and carriers spread out and then fired at those they were up against as they came from many different angles.

Heturadi knew he would have to commit more fighters to the battle to win without sustaining more losses than he was prepared to accept. Just before he ordered some carriers farther behind his ship, which was barely being attacked, to launch their fighters, new Lutresas and Reduzen carriers came out of hyperlight speed along with carriers from both races' main fleets. These carriers had more veteran pilots, and they wanted to test Heturadi. The fleet commander was well aware of their capabilities. The Lutresas carriers were blue and dark green. They looked like long, rectangular, wide pipes with extra black metallic shield plating where the bridge area was. The ship's bay doors were black and thick. They were incredibly hard to destroy and were a scavenger salvage crew's dream. The brown and dark blue Reduzen carriers looked like two long, wide cylinders with a sleek, pointed bow and stern end with powerful propulsion systems powering the ships, which moved quickly in all directions.

The war had not reached the planet yet, where the main battle was due to begin. Still, Heturadi was determined to clear a path and get

Vatemfa's gladiators to their destination. He was ready to do whatever it took to get to Qukosi, and death was everywhere already. This was going to be the fleet commander's hardest journey yet. Still, he knew victory was inevitable as the captains in the cruisers and carriers around him instinctively ordered fire. The enemy's ships were almost stopped dead in their tracks. The apparent loss of life was never going to stop Heturadi from pushing forward. His mission was to strengthen the Kalicos empire for his king and secure his future within the Kalicos hierarchy as he fought to strengthen the empire he served.

Chapter Twelve

Fasjey sat and waited to speak to the Lutresas queen in the hall of blessed warrior souls in her main palace. Her royal guards stood all around her as Jarkepe walked into the hall and bowed his head slightly. Queen Fasjey tilted her head and touched her neck.

"I have pains in my body from worrying about the attack on Qukosi," she said.

"Soon, we will see whether Queen Xunaseta is prepared for the coming war, Your Majesty, Jarkepe said. "The invasion fleet may reach Qukosi, and the Kalicos gladiator legions campaign could last for days."

The sensors on the wall before Fasjey beeped, and the queen readied herself to converse with her ally in the war against the Kalicos king.

"Xunaseta is always ready, Jarkepe. She has fought in wars before. Now, we will hear the queen's thoughts and give her our support," Fasjey said.

The sensor scanned Fasjey and Jarkepe, and then Xunaseta's holographic image appeared on a flat circular panel on the floor in the court just in front of the wall.

"Hello, Queen Fasjey," Xunaseta said.

Fasjey smiled. "Gracious queen and friend of mine. How are you in these dangerous times?"

"I am feeling the pressure as the threat from King Grandres's forces is real, and he has no intention of letting my race survive. I have heard from certain traders that he even approached the clone barons and told them we would be a race they could use to rebuild their empire once he had finished with us. Rikshaz, the god of all the planetary systems, will punish the Kalicos nation one day as he did in the past by making Zetrax, their old home world, a planet filled with death and destruction."

Fasjey felt that she and Xunaseta would always share the same concerns. "We will always have a powerful bond that helps us shape the nations we control. One day, our allies will be ready for the uprising. I have sent you as many ships as I can. Every warrior beast I have sent to Qukosi will fight to the death. More ships will be sent every day from the Giyehe engineers. They build ships even faster than the Yatavra engineers ever could."

"Thank you, warrior queen, greatest of all my allies," Xunaseta said. "I will always remember our friendship no matter what happens."

"Have no fear, Queen Xunaseta," Fasjey said.

"I know that if the blood legions fight us on Qukosi soil, they will quickly meet their match when they face the war breeders' best. Your beast warriors fight with us on the front lines and protect the old cities as we speak. We will prevail."

"I know that you will. I believe in you."

Jarkepe walked as the sensor scanned him. He came into view for Xunaseta and bowed his head quickly again.

"Your Majesty, I am sure your fleet commander, Mewetesi, the baron slayer, has been informed of the fleet of hunter cruisers and carriers we have sent to the planets you control. Fleet Commander Ujesal will defend the planets where our clones are made to the best of his ability."

"Thank you, Jarkepe; I have sent the largest fleet Mewetesi could muster to my planets where the Lutresas citizens enjoy entertainment. Many who were enjoying the delights on the surface of these planets know what is coming, and we must protect them at all costs."

Jarkepe's voice became severe, "I have told my beast master what I expect from the Gazaxa warrior beasts. They will secure victory for us all wherever they fight the enemy."

"My breed of killers has been patrolling the planet in large hordes," Xunaseta said. "I am confident that the genetics chambers have produced the best kind of warrior to use in a war of this kind. My scientists and generals have promised me this."

Queen Fasjey speaks far more severely than Jarkepe, "I am pleased that you have produced the finest breed possible to enhance our chances of a swift victory in the face of adversity. History shall be made today. Perhaps today, the Blood Legions will be eradicated by the thousands."

Jarkepe tilted his head towards the ground, "I have all the time in the world to wait for the intergalactic gladiator Blood Legions to be vanquished. For over a thousand cycles, they have slain many brave souls."

Fasjey almost screamed but restrained herself. "Grandres will soon witness the demise of his son and the rest of his lineage."

"I will follow your example as a strong queen of the most blessed race, Fasjey, for I wish to see the Lutresas flourish wherever they may be. Now, I must depart. My generals require my presence at their side. Farewell."

"I shall converse with you when the light of day graces Qukosi's sandy shores," Fasjey stated.

Fasjey turned to Jarkepe once Xunaseta's hologram had disappeared. "I wish to speak with Ujesal as soon as possible, Jarkepe."

"Yes, Your Majesty," the ready and able general replied.

Fasjey exited the room with the queen's guard, and Jarkepe stood, observing them as they marched in unison. He was confident that the queen would instruct Ujesal to be prepared to unite with all her allies and that it was time to devise a comprehensive battle plan, readying them for any conflict with the Yatavra-System Lords. Soon, he would fulfil his destiny and challenge one of the mightiest forces in any galaxy.

Chapter Thirteen

Seventy Yatavra military guards marched with Hetkarej into the royal petal fields of Etrehen in the capital of Dortizal. The fields were owned by the grand lord master, who possessed a palace fit for any system lord with power and wealth at his level. Mocowas had permitted Gorxab to retain much of what he had owned in terms of residences as a former prince. Gorxab's sister, Mirehesa's garden workers, scattered petals on the fields every summer, ensuring the grass was always covered. The scent of the planet's most beautiful flowers lingered in the air whenever the system lord was home. The palace boasted numerous pillars aligned beneath tall gem-covered archways and a partially bronze-plated white stone roof. The main roof was shaped like half of a pumpkin, while the other two roofs on either side of the main roof were pointed and appeared spiralled at the top. The stained-glass windows depicted the ascendancy of the system of lords, showcasing different important rulers who were the regimental geniuses shaping the Yatavra race. The palace's design, based on old traditional aesthetics, never mattered to Gorxab as long as he lived the best life.

Hetkarej smiled as he walked atop the light purple and sky-blue petals. It was easy to see why the royal family cherished their lives so much and relished that they could not be entirely removed from the seat of power. The citizens on every planet where Yatavra citizens resided believed that the Jowekre family should be treated with respect and afforded the best treatment. They might have been accused of trying to entangle the empire in political controversy with new values that many citizens didn't care for, but they did not deserve imprisonment. They constructed a great empire to be both admired and feared. Hetkarej understood this well; the citizens had witnessed the royal family being overthrown by Mocowas and never rebelled. The supreme lord conveyed to the masses a need for change so things would remain as they were for the foreseeable future.

Hetkarej gazed across the field and saw Gorxab beyond the open gates of the twenty-five-foot rear wall to his palace. The masterful system lord observed five topless Yatavra males and females bathing each other in a perfume-filled pool with large shells. The muscular females squealed with delight as they touched and kissed each other sensually. The men became aroused and began to touch and kiss the females. Gorxab leered at the females as he sipped his pink-coloured syrup with water and ate Yatavra yellow fruit in between. He enjoyed the company of his friends, and he had many females to satisfy his needs. Known to be incredibly virile, Gorxab was once wild but had ceased obsessing over being the most adventurous among his friends. Yet, he still preferred his partners to approach him when it came to using sex to pass the time.

Hetkarej approached the palace, walking past the twelve guards at the gate who neither flinched nor seemed to notice or care about the small orgy unfolding before their eyes.

Gorxab grinned and placed his drink and fruit down on a golden tray. "Hetkarej, it's good you are here," he said. "Why did you not bring Ralshafa?"

Hetkarej glanced at the female, who stared at him and waved. "She has encountered numerous problems with the renegade force in every sector her new fleet has patrolled. Suppose she does not secure the region in space that we use as a route to the new colonies. If we fail to protect what is ours in certain systems, there will be a problem building new cities for the clone barons to work on our next generation of armies."

Gorxab walked up to the pool and touched one of the females on the cheek. "Mocowas was wise to align the clone barons on our side again after all this time," he said. "They mostly keep to themselves. The Supreme Lord Master knows they will significantly add to the empire. By getting them to create our new soldiers, he ensures his legacy will be seen as that of a leader who seeks only to make us an unstoppable force that will rival any renegade, be they scavenger or pirate, who claims they can defeat us in space or on the battlefield."

Hetkarej felt he should respect Mocowas's decision as he had earned at least that much from him. The clone barons opposed the System Lords' reign when they reached for the stars and began to build their own intergalactic empire until the Lutresas military defeated them.

"I think Mocowas will hand over his power to Esekal soon after we win the war against the renegade force," he said.

Gorxab walked away from the side of his pool, picked up his wine, and drank slowly.

"Come with me, Hetkarej."

The two System Lords entered the palace and sat on a long silver chair resembling thick vines with flowers. Gorxab finished his drink, and a maid dressed in grey and white see-through material took it away.

Hetkarej spoke freely, as he always did around Gorxab, "Esekal will not be able to match Mocowas's absolute strength."

"Unless she starts to build on his empire, and I think that will happen. Mocowas knows it, and so do you, Hetkarej."

Hetkarej became frustrated and began to feel a headache coming on. "I want to kill her before she assumes the seat of power."

Gorxab smiled. "Never aim too high, Hetkarej. When I told you many want you to attain the seat of power, I knew it would be achievable, but not like that. At least not for now."

"I need to know I can carry out my plans without being hindered by a Supreme Lord who will wage a private vendetta against me, Gorxab. Mocowas trained Esekel, and he wants me out of the way. If he cannot achieve this, his former protégé will."

Gorxab's face showed concern. "Mocowas detests you, but he cannot act on his hatred in an obvious way. You know this, yet you show fear in front of me now. Why?"

Hetkarej was quick to answer with a serious tone, "I feel Mocowas will want to clear the path for Esekal to do as she pleases concerning all that I own and control, so he will dispose of me for her or make sure she does it quickly during her reign."

Gorxab rang a small bell on a wooden and golden table before him. "You are becoming paranoid, but maybe that will keep your senses sharp and aware, my friend," he said. "Just don't succumb to fear. Nobody must know you would kill a Supreme Lord to get what you want. We will never speak of this again."

A female servant wore a beautiful black and grey robe made of delicate, expensive material with a white sash. Gorxab looked at her as if she were attractive. He touched the servant's hand when she stood next to him.

"Bring me some stew. Ensure there is more meat than chopped-up green roots in the mine. Bring a fish stew for Lord Hetkarej." Gorxab looked at the Yatavra thinker, whom he would always support. "I know how much you enjoy cooked fish stew, Hetkarej."

"Let us discuss our plan to make Grandres support us rather than oppose us."

"Hetkarej, I'm telling you, do not play a dangerous game with Grandres without me. He will decimate Xunaseta's military, and the victory will make him sharper than ever."

"I already know this and will be ready to offer him a deal to keep him satisfied if necessary. Remember, Esekal is all set to take over, and she favours the Reduzen queen, much like her most ardent supporter, Grand Lord Master Pakowe. As long as Queen Fasjey stays in line, they will choose her over Grandres. There is more for you to worry about than we originally planned, as the renegade forces have become more than a thorn in our side. Their battle with the Borshux miners has empowered them, and they smell blood, seeking victory in battle across many galaxies."

Focus your mind, Hetkarej. Do not let anything weaken you. Later, we will go over some strategies. But before we do that, we must entertain ourselves. I saw a beautiful female staring at you earlier. Time to prove yourself to her, and I will take my two favourite lovers to my chambers after I eat and have some naughty fun. I am not how I used to be as a Yatvra powerhouse, but I still have quite the appetite when it comes to the fairer sex."

Hetkarej almost laughed as he observed the beautiful friends Gorxab had invited to his palace, and they frolicked outside naked. They ran back and forth as they screamed and shouted. He ogled the females and allowed himself to forget about his worries. But he was fully aware that when all was said and done, he would start to think about his future and the paranoia that had entered his soul ever since the war with the renegade forces began. He would always have to defend his actions and ensure any schemes he came up with got him everything he wanted without making him enemies within his ranks. Mocowas would watch his System Lords' every action more than usual to ensure everyone reached their true potential. This was one of the most important times in Hetkarej's life, and he could not afford to make a mistake as this would cost him dearly.

Chapter Fourteen

Lutresas carriers and cruisers were poised for the heavyweights' battle to begin. Fleet Commander Mewetesi had felt that the war between the Kalicos and the Lutresas would become the sole topic of conversation across thousands of planets for many cycles to come. The Reduzen beast carriers were expected to arrive any minute. Each carrier transported hundreds of the legendary, unbeatable warriors of their day. Soon, the Lutresas slayers would stand alongside the Gazaxa beasts in their thousands.

Mewetesi was an imposing figure with strong cheekbones and a quite wide jaw. Slight wrinkles marked her forehead, and her dark hair was longer than usual, cascading down her back to a quarter way down her crimson red blazer, which featured a dark grey collar. She had a medium build and was well-toned, with recognisable features like most who had assumed the role of fleet commander in the past, as demanded by Queen Xunaseta's mother, Acaxantil, when she was alive. Acaxantil insisted that all superiors of the Lutresas race must present themselves in this manner. She favoured a clean-cut commander who was physically attractive and presentable, believing it would aid their ascent to true power amongst the elite on her planet and others she controlled where her kind resided. The superiors in the Lutresas race looked completely different from the lower class. They were bred to look aesthetically beautiful in many instances. They were hybrid clones, with certain races whose gifted features were spoken of throughout many galaxies being part of the mix when it came to the creative process. Scientists worked hard to make them stand out and were trained to be exemplary in everything.

The fleet commander felt confident yet cautious. Mewetesi couldn't help but ponder the consequences of losing the war. Aware that such thoughts could be perceived as fear, she quickly closed her blue/green eyes, attempted to clear her mind, mentally reviewed battle tactics, and reopened her eyes.

Mewetesi stood steadfast on her battle carrier, observing space through the view screen. She was ready to fulfil her queen's commands despite feeling cold and dark. Mewetesi had always been prepared to serve, coming from a family of males who were all distinguished fighters in the military. With legends in her lineage, who all started from the bottom just as she had, she now, as a legend herself, must take another step forward and confront whatever lay ahead.

The Reduzen beast carriers arrived punctually. The ships were a striking grey with Tethaka beasts depicted on their sides like emblems. Two large pieces of metal, shaped like horns and placed upside down on either side of the gargantuan vessels, made them uniquely distinguishable. Massive passenger shuttles with powerful propulsion capabilities immediately emerged from the ships once the bay doors opened, descending towards the planet in groups of thirty. These shuttles landed all over the planet, with hundreds more carriers continually arriving and departing. The Reduzen queen had bred countless beasts on many planets far from Daheza. Mocowas had always believed they might prove useful one day. Still, he had failed to monitor the calculating queen closely, allowing the number of beasts at her disposal to grow exponentially. With the queen's permission, many others used them for protection. This situation concerned many leaders who would pressure the System Lords to eliminate the beasts should they begin feeling threatened. This worried Fasjey, but not enough to halt her orders for Oshdan to continue breeding as many beasts as possible.

Mewetesi settled into the fleet commander's chair, bracing herself. Given the Kalicos fleets' attacks on all fronts, it was clear that the space battle near the planet could commence at any moment. Three separate fleets were now advancing on the planet. The enemy deployed their fighters like long-range scouting ships that attacked in large waves, exerting immense pressure on the Lutresas pilots. The Kalicos fought with terrifying ferocity when inflamed by the rage of harsh conditions, a tactic Heturadi would not hesitate to employ in a deadly war.

A pilot called out to Mewetesi, "Fleet Commander Ujesal is on the communications link."

Sensors flashed white on the ship's wall, and a holographic projection of Ujesal appeared—the all-powerful fleet commander who always liked to make his presence felt stood tall and proud.

"Mewetesi, I am sending more cruisers to systems that must have regular patrols in the region," Ujesal said. "We are giving you these ships to win this war. The new cruisers we are sending will also come to planet Qukosi, and the cruisers that will support your fighters carry the new revolving laser rail cannons with plasma torpedo port attachments. These weapons use extra metallic shield plates. Do not fail us. Live up to the Yosuntuk family name. Understand, you are my equal, but you are facing a fleet commander with more experience than us. He has seen many wars like this in his time."

Mewetesi forced a smile on her face, feeling as if Ujesal was trying to impart lessons. "I am aware of the enemy's capabilities and will ensure my kind fight with courage and honour. I am sure you are just as prepared as I am for what comes next. We killed many during the first major encounter. We slowed down Heturadi, whose attackers still engage in close combat battles with our fighters. His fleet was slowed at first, then split up, and with some parts of it regrouping at new coordinates, they disappeared quickly before our ships arrived. We expect the two main groups of ships from the fleet that went into hyperdrive before we could catch them to be here soon. Our planet's defences are ready, including the plasma torpedo stations and laser cannon space stations the Giyehe engineers built for us. We will survive and prosper after this bloody mess is over."

"I will listen out for any updates. If you succeed, we will celebrate together on Qukosi and enjoy a fine feast, Fleet Commander Mewetesi. Goodbye."

The hologram ceased projecting. Mewetesi noted the ship's scanners showed even more carriers had arrived. They were waiting on standby at a further distance from the planet. They carried additional Gazaxa beasts. Mewetesi had heard that Queen Fasjey had told Queen Xunaseta it was clear that her beasts and the Lutresas army would fight like true blood-crazed slayers. It was necessary to bring them together. This would be a perfect moment to witness their combined battlefield forces in action, and defeating Vatemfa's intergalactic gladiator blood legions would secure the warrior queen's place in history. Fasjey had passed the age where she could be on the battlefield herself, but she still craved blood and loved hearing stories about flesh being burnt off by the heat of laser gunfire. The blood legions must fall and never rise when they set foot on the planet's surface if this war was to be won.

Mewetesi saw the ships at a further distance release their passenger shuttles, which flew down to the planet's surface. She turned to the communications operator.

"Tell the captains on those carriers to expedite the transport of the Gazaxa beasts to the planet," she instructed.

"Yes, fleet commander," the communications operator replied.

The large group of cruisers that Ujesal had informed Mewetesi about arrived. The space around the planet was crowded, but this was necessary, and everything had been meticulously planned.

Mewetesi stood up. "Inform the captains of half of the cruisers to proceed to the coordinates we send them."

She then addressed her onboard strategic team. "Work to ascertain where the Reduzen cruisers should be directed immediately. I want a report on the whereabouts of our defensive fighters who went out on patrol. The enemy will arrive any moment now. I can feel it."

Just as the last few passenger shuttles left the carriers at breakneck speeds in larger groups at high speeds, the first Kalicos ships that had broken away from the main fleet emerged from hyperdrive near the planet. The Lutresas carriers and sensors detected this, compelling Mewetesi to devise tactics to reassure her crew of her readiness. The veteran fleet commander had to demonstrate her capability to outmanoeuvre the enemy, as the finest leaders always lead by example.

As Mewetesi observed more passenger shuttles descending to the planet's surface, she resumed her seat. Then, without warning, hundreds of Kalicos close combat vessels exited at hyper-light speed and attacked the passenger shuttles, the first apparent targets in their sights. The fighters patrolling the space around the planet engaged the Kalicos attackers. The defensive strategy was to entangle the attackers in fast-paced close combat, distracting them from the shuttles. The Reduzen cruisers retaliated against the attackers, destroying them in large numbers. Suddenly, the remainder of the fleet appeared, fully prepared for war. Despite the grim situation, Mewetesi remained composed, her fearlessness evident.

Lutresas carriers advanced towards the main fleet, approaching the planet at normal impulse speeds before halting and unleashing a torrent of attackers. Additional patrolling fighters converged with the carriers. Some carriers closer to Qukosi opened their bay doors, releasing over two thousand fighters into space. The Lutresas cruisers unleashed their formidable laser cannons and missiles, targeting critical areas on the Kalicos' larger vessels. The attackers targeted the core of the Lutresas vessels in large swarms. Despite significant damage, the older, smaller carriers managed to deploy vast swarms of attackers before drifting aimlessly in space after sustaining missile fire from the Kalicos cruisers.

The ensuing close combat battle was chaotic. The fighters' pilots, determined to defend their homeland, clashed with attackers driven by a destructive mindset, intent on inflicting maximum damage. This confrontation promised to be a war of the most graphic and horrendous nature for all involved. Hundreds of attackers targeted Mewetesi's battle carrier, prompting the deployment of its formidable arsenal. The launched missiles intercepted many attackers, resulting in a series of explosions that illuminated the darkness of space. Some attackers and debris impacted the robust plating shielding the bridge area of the battle carrier. Mewetesi, witnessing this on the view screen, felt her heart rate accelerate with every flicker of light and spark off the metal plating. The attackers focused on the passenger shuttles, firing their lasers to destroy them. Despite their strength, these ships were vulnerable to sustained attacks. Each Reduzen beast carrier deployed its contingent of fighters, which immediately engaged the enemy upon reaching firing range.

The Reduzen fighters targeted the attackers' cockpits, aiming to inflict maximum harm. This relentless pursuit of suffering seemed eternal to both adversaries. Many realms anticipated this moment, knowing that the war's outcome would preoccupy the leaders of the involved races long after its conclusion. Without the System Lords' intervention, the aftermath could trigger another extensive conflict among allies.

Not all Kalicos attackers employed evasive combat manoeuvres, and their determination to halt the passenger shuttles was unwavering. They breached many shuttle hulls with laser fire, coinciding with the plasma torpedo stations' arrival in the heavily contested space region. The Reduzen fighters targeted every attacker within range, shooting them down as the crew on the plasma torpedo station meticulously selected their targets. They launched as many torpedoes as possible, observing as the auburn and white lights illuminated space's dark, cold expanse.

Mewetesi addressed the communications operator, stating, "Inform the other battle carriers to deploy the fighters equipped with missile capabilities. I want them to fully engage the Kalicos carriers and cruisers and determine when the remaining Reduzen fighters will arrive."

"I will issue the order immediately, fleet commander," the operator responded.

Mewetesi harboured concerns that the remaining carriers might not reach Qukosi to deliver the Gazaxa beasts.

The Lutresas battle carriers opened their bay doors, releasing a flood of fighters. They activated their lasers almost instantly upon exiting, clearing virtually all the space ahead.

Mewetesi issued another directive, "Instruct the captains of five of our carriers to have their fighters encircle the Reduzen beast carriers and the passenger shuttles as they depart, offering them the best protection possible."

The operator nodded, affirming, "Yes, fleet commander."

As the operator relayed the instruction, Mewetesi said, "Advise the Reduzen fleet to request additional cruisers."

The operator relayed, "I've just received a message from a Reduzen cruiser captain. He informs me that fighters from three systems are en route and should arrive shortly."

The Lutresas fighters, armed with missiles, approached the Kalicos main fleet. At the same time, those guarding the Reduzen carriers engaged the Kalicos attackers, targeting the passenger shuttles. Some shuttles exploded as they entered Qukosi's atmosphere, struck by multiple laser cannon shots. Hundreds of attackers, launched from their carriers, approached the fighters at alarming speeds, opening fire simultaneously. Missiles and laser beams intersected. Some laser shots from the attackers detonated the missiles prematurely. In contrast, others struck their targets or missed, speeding past to hit a few Kalicos carriers and cruisers too slow to intercept them with their lasers.

The battle between the fighters and attackers occurred perilously close to the Kalicos cruisers, eliminating many Lutresas fighters in small clusters. The fighters charged towards the cruisers in large formations, launching missiles and firing lasers to disable their cannons or damage their missile platforms. Subsequently, hundreds of fighters withdrew to the battle carriers to reload with a new arsenal of missiles, each fighter carrying twelve missiles. The Lutresas cruisers advanced to engage directly, covering the retreating fighters. Having left the Reduzen hunter cruisers to counter the attackers targeting the passenger shuttles, it was their turn to inflict significant damage on a formidable adversary. Anticipating that the attackers would pursue the retreating fighters, the cruiser captains prepared a robust barrage of firepower as their fighters passed by and re-entered the battle carriers. The attackers endured substantial losses, their aggression leading to a devastating defeat. Numerous Kalicos pilots perished. In retaliation, the Kalicos carriers launched a massive missile salvo, directing over two thousand missiles towards the Lutresas cruisers and carriers. The planet's laser cannon stations sprang into action, ready to defend against the onslaught. Five colossal, monster-looking flying vessels opened fire from their position alongside the Lutresas vessels. Their extra-long, wide laser cannons, equipped with five or six barrels, could fire short or long bursts as required. Hundreds of missiles were swiftly shot down, but many struck fighters and attackers engaged in close combat, as well as the Lutresas cruisers and carriers. The nearby Reduzen cruisers were also hit. Some stray missiles impacted the last few passenger shuttles heading towards the planet. Each shuttle carried forty Gazaxa beasts, and hundreds of small vessels had reached the surface before the Kalico's main fleet arrived. However, a significant number of warriors were lost in the attack.

 Mewetesi was concerned that not enough beasts had made it to the planet. The war breeders had produced two million warriors to defend the megacities on the Lutresas homeworld, including the capital city, Owakwon, with another million protecting the outskirts of all cities. Additionally, half a million more warriors were dispersed in each important region far from any city. There were also almost four hundred and fifty thousand Gazaxa beasts on the planet's surface, positioned in various locations, safeguarding the most critical military facilities where their prowess as fierce and feared fighters was needed most. Heturadi and Vatemfa had arranged for hundreds of thousands of intergalactic gladiators to be brought to the planet over time. These forces were being transported on many fleets that travelled separately, not counting the gladiators who had already accompanied them. Mewetesi was aware of ships in other systems poised to enter hyper-light drive speed to bring the gladiators to Qukosi. Jarkepe had cautioned the heroic fleet commander that Vatemfa would keep his elite forces on standby in a planetary system controlled by the Kalicos, ready for combat, in addition to at least two more fleets comprising different types of blood legion gladiators, from veterans to the youth core, stationed elsewhere, separate from the other gladiators. Vatemfa regularly employed these tactics in general. His well-trained fighters would all land after the space battle concluded. The Kalicos fleet commander had targeted bombings where he suspected the most damage could be inflicted on cities where citizens and military bases were defended. The intergalactic gladiators were killing machines at their core, murderers through and through. Mewetesi needed to thwart any major assault on Lutresas soil that could jeopardise Xunaseta's reign.

Mewetesi knew that one hundred thousand more beasts would arrive in carriers over the next few days, and thousands more ships were en route to join the battle. Kalicos carriers would attempt to deploy countless hordes of gladiators.

Mewetesi glanced at her strategists and almost frowned. "What must we do to prevent the Kalicos fleets from delivering the invading force to their final destination?"

One of the strategists looked up and replied, "The ships will be challenging to defeat even if we can separate the fleet. Simply trying to divide and conquer, as they are adept at, will not suffice. Heturadi's ship must be destroyed, and the Reduzen ships must attack as many gladiator carriers as possible, fleet commander."

Doing as much territorial damage as possible was all Heturadi aimed to achieve. Mewetesi and her strategists had devised a plan to tackle every battle as it arose. Nonetheless, Heturadi would strive to conclude this battle swiftly to witness Xunaseta's downfall. Mewetesi was eager to prove herself, fully aware that it would be an uphill struggle for her and the crews under her command.

Chapter Fifteen

Several dozen Giyehe politicians stood in the temple of the gods on Kretaq in Takizde, one of the main cities of worship. They waved their hands in the air, shouting and hollering. Dekrehas raised his hand, and they fell silent. He stood on a large marble-looking pulpit in the middle of the temple, holding a light metallic object sculpted to resemble a silver-coloured scroll with a gold seal. Dekrehas's finger rubbed back and forth over it, akin to a child with a lucky gemstone. This object symbolised the leader of the Giyehe race's authority in the political world he controlled.

"We all know that soon we will be at war, whether we like it or not, as Mocowas undoubtedly feels we will become a great threat to him and his race if we work with our many allies and join the renegade forces who oppose him. I hear that Yatavra fleets are patrolling every system they can to find and eliminate every pirate and scavenger possible. They want to wipe them out."

The temple erupted; Dekrehas raised both hands, silencing the politicians around him.

"We will hear some words from our top general soon, and he will tell us his plans," Dekrehas said. "I can tell you that he is ready for an attack, and we will support Queen Fasjey and our other allies. We will defend them at all costs, and the leaders of all the nations that support us have told me they will do whatever it takes to win, no matter the cost. We must succeed in our endeavours; sometimes, we must suffer to grow. Here is General Wesyal's update on our activities here and worldwide."

General Wesyal stood up on a pulpit at the back of the temple. The line of metallic cream seats and benches facing Dekrehas moved forward while the pulpit the prime architect stood on also hovered to the side. Once it stopped moving, Dekrehas stepped off it with the help of a young temple guard. He then sat on a golden-coloured bench with platinum-looking armrests, now re-positioned at ground level closer to the pulpit where Wesyal stood.

Wesyal appeared stern, ready for any argument or battle. A seasoned veteran and a born fighter, he was considered an incredible anomaly who should never have survived the attacks he faced in numerous incredible battles his race had fought on enemy land over the last forty cycles.

"As a general, it is my responsibility to protect the people. I will be honest with all of you. I feel this will be a war that shakes us to our very core. Many of you will sometimes sleep at night feeling frightened and worried. I hope that, at some point, this will pass. Over the next few days, the streets will be filled with guards on every corner, patrolling every road and street. This is a closed session, so the citizens will not officially know why this is happening, but they are not fooling. Some who travel off the planet have spoken many truths and will never stop spreading rumours about a pending war between the Yatavra- System Lords and us. The military is ready to mobilise on all fronts. Planet security has always been on the agenda, and Prime Architect Dekrehas supports all my initiatives. We will step up sky patrols night and day. Fleet Commander Paltovis has overseen the construction of off-world security stations linked to our space stations and border patrol bases. These security stations can move freely, though slower than the cannon and torpedo stations that protect the planet. They are gargantuan, and the flow of security ships in every area of space we control will improve. Regulation is key from now on. Many ships can be launched from these stations, and new ones are being built, which will eventually be the size of large cities. This will be a sight to behold. The Yatavra has met their match, even if they have not realised it yet."

The politicians cheer and clap their hands, and Wesyal grins to show his approval. Wesyal's grin becomes laughter. He then stands still and raises one hand calmly.

"Our relationship with the Reduzen race grows stronger daily, and Queen Fasjey supports us with all her heart and soul. Fleet Commander Paltovis ensures that all the cruisers and carriers are built at their right destinations. He will be ordered to meet with Fleet Commander Mewetesi at some point to assist her in protecting Lutresa strongholds if she fares well after the attack on Qukosi. Once the war has started, we must get used to relying on each other's tactics and using valuable information to our advantage. There are many systems over which the Yatavra have no control. We will make new allies and form a powerful alliance with the Lutresas as they seek to build a stronger army. Xunaseta gave orders for a few scientists to be hidden from the world, and she was smart to do so. We will help finance the Lutresas race, and they will become even stronger, with Mewetesi guiding a new mega fleet. Alpha Guardian Boprexu will lead the Lutresas race if the queen cannot. You can all be assured that our nations' bond will last for many cycles."

The politicians clap and cheer again, and then Wesyal speaks loudly. "We have millions of guards on the planet, and we are continuously adding to the numbers in the army. There are hundreds of thousands of ships at our disposal, and we have built at least that many over just ten cycles with the help of more than one race. If we keep pushing, we may eventually be able to compete with the Yatavra race, which has built an all-conquering fleet. The task is to stop them from gaining even more allies than they already have from wanting to join any intergalactic war. Many Kings, Emperors, and Empresses have not agreed to be in any war. We can win this war without heavy casualties if we get just a few rulers. Suppose we cannot gain them as allies. In that case, the war will last as long as you have heard—anything from three to five cycles based on the strategists' calculations, and that is if we can withstand the pressure our fighting forces face. I must tell you I have been told by more than a few of our top strategists that the war could last longer."

At this precise moment, Dekrehas stood up. Many of the male and female politicians were talking and whispering. As Dekrehas stood on the pulpit, it floated until he was at eye level with some who sat on the higher benches.

He spoke in a strong, commanding voice, "I ask you, my friends and trusted advisors, to be strong and pray," he said. "We will never see a day without the Yatavra trying to squeeze the life and soul out of less powerful races all over the universe in a cruel future over countless cycles if we do not face some hardships here in the present. Now, let us debate what we must tell our citizens. They need to know where we stand eventually. We are a proud and bold race of hard workers and our kind fight battles together. This is how it will be forever, as our ancestors stated when we were the strongest race."

Chapter Sixteen

Yatavra servants set a long table with cutlery for two. Hetkarej and Ralshafa watched them from an adjoining room. They enjoyed yellow fruit and hot buns while drinking wine from the royal vineyards just outside one of the former king's palaces, which the System Lords now used as a haven and base of operations. As Hetkarej sipped his wine, he organised his thoughts. He was due to converse with Grandres after dinner and aimed for a focused and clear mind. The all-conquering king was known for his cunning and mastery of deception. As the leader of his race, he was committed to prioritising their interests. Mocowas had made it clear to Hetkarej that handling Grandres was his responsibility, and any misstep by Grandres would be Hetkarej's fault. Aware of this, Hetkarej intended to offer his support to the king of the Kalicos nation, hoping to prove himself a reliable ally under specific conditions that he planned to clarify to ensure both understood their mutual standings.

Ralshafa finished her wine in a tall green glass and mentioned, "Grandres, the brute of Bretasi, is frustrated he cannot attack Queen Fasjey on a planet where they both reside."

Hetkarej, picking at his yellow fruit on a small pink and gold plate, responded, "I have dispatched thousands of soldiers from the Yatavra clone army to guard the borders. Mocowas has instructed me to send another hundred thousand as the sun sets today, and I will comply. He intends to thwart the great king and demonstrate that, as the Supreme Lord Master, he governs at his discretion, even if it means restricting the Kalicos gladiators' movements against Queen Fasjey's Gazaxa warrior beasts."

After contemplating, Ralshafa added, "Fasjey will urge her allies to eliminate every Kalicos if possible as the Lutresas empire faces destruction. Soon, this war will extend to the territories of planet Daheza."

"Mocowas will lose control if that occurs, then look to me to solve any arising issue," Hetkarej remarked. "He is preoccupied with the renegade force and is determined to eradicate them permanently."

Ralshafa glanced at a servant approaching her, then turned back to Hetkarej, "The supreme lord will also hold you responsible if the war escalates and triggers a different kind of uprising."

Hetkarej, visibly frustrated, acknowledged, "You speak the truth, Ralshafa. Many races aspire to usurp our position of power across the galaxies. We cannot afford to relinquish it."

The approaching servant halted before Ralshafa, announcing, "Lord Ralshafa, the table is prepared."

Ralshafa, with a firm tone, replied, "I will join the table shortly." As the servant walked away, she refilled her wine glass from a small bottle. "You will accompany me to dinner, of course?"

Feeling an overwhelming need to speak with King Grandres first and not in the mood to eat, Hetkarej stood up, stating, "I will see you after I have dealt with King Grandres."

Ralshafa offered a smile and proceeded to the dining room without further comment.

Hetkarej turned and went to the holo-comm rooms in another palace section. He passed through several spacious lounges where Yatavra-System Lords were entertained by the most beautiful humanoid females from a broad expanse of space. The females acted as if they adored and worshipped both male and female System Lords, a tactic to satisfy the dominant leaders. Hetkarej, distracted by the sounds of his peers indulging in pleasures, hastened past the room until the noise faded, refocusing on the upcoming discussion with King Grandres.

Hetkarej reached the holo-comm room, which he would use to contact Grandres. Upon entering the spacious area, a guard inside the doorway closed a white double door with a brown handle and drew a red curtain across it. A communications operator stood by a panel on a tall pedestal, pressing a touchscreen as soon as Hetkarej positioned himself across from the wall sensors. The guard stepped aside. Hetkarej prepared himself as the communication link connected with planet Daheza, where Grandres was preparing for the harvest festival.

Grandres answered the call, adorned in purple robes with a grey sash; his head was crowned with gold and adorned with a design resembling silver thorns featuring various coloured gems above it. Many former Kalicos tribes had surrounded their villages on planet Zetrax, the old homeworld, with poisonous thorn flowers to protect against less intelligent, vicious predators.

Grandres smiled, placing his hand on his sash. "Hello, Hetkarej. I am about to observe the preparations for the parade, starting with the sunrise in Bretasi. I may celebrate another planet-wide victory in a few days as we plan to invade planet Qukosi and defeat the Lutresas queen, Xunaseta."

"That may be your outcome, Grandres, but retaliation could lead one race to obliterate another, costing millions of lives. The Reduzen empire extends to the far reaches of space, and like you, Queen Fasjey has many allies. They will react fiercely if pushed, and I believe they will."

"My allies will seek retribution if all is lost for me and my kingdom," Grandres countered.

"Then, you must collaborate with the System Lords to prevent any escalation, win or lose. Join us and combat the renegade force, Grandres. Your experience is invaluable. Imagine the possibilities if you resolved your differences with Queen Fasjey. You could revive your empire to legendary status, and the legacy you leave would be unparalleled."

"I've heard Mocowas failed to locate the renegade force at the coordinates where leaders were supposed to meet with scavengers from distant systems. It could have been a trap, or the meeting could have occurred elsewhere. If I had the time, I would assist you with this issue. However, the Reduzen have declared my kind their enemy. I am compelled to see them suffer and perish by every means my gladiators can enact."

"Soon, Mocowas will grow weary of your actions and discipline you and Fasjey. He might seize all you cherish as a reminder of the Supreme Lord Master's ultimate authority. You may think he's playing a complex game, but his intention is for you to understand and heed his directives."

Grandres's arrogance was evident in his response, "Mocowas is oblivious to the paranoia pervading the citizens of Bretasi and the fear my adversaries seek to instil in those I safeguard. Those descended from conquerors are destined to engage in every conflict as their predecessors did, ensuring they never succumb to the throne's most formidable contenders."

Hetkarej smiled. "The life of a king is never supposed to be easy, but then, I do not need to tell you this, Grandres. You once spoke to me of the moment you first heard the words' Your Majesty' and understood their meaning for the first time and how the responsibilities you faced became clear."

"Now I am faced with an impossible decision, Hetkarej. I must end this war and seek victory across the galaxy wherever the Reduzen bloodlines exist. Where Fasjey's supporters are, they will perish. If Mocowas insists on limiting my strikes on this planet, then so be it, but I must defend my interests to the world. I have made my statement and a true king must stand by his words for as long as he lives."

"I will relay these words to Mocowas, King of Daheza. Perhaps he will not become unsettled if he benefits from the invasion of Qukosi. My advice is to ensure that he does. The Lutresas race is not his favourite, but his apparent lack of control would make him seem weak if he had not just brokered a new deal with the clone barons to create the Yatavra, a new breed of warriors. If you emerge victorious, the wealth accrues to Mocowas may mitigate any future challenges you face, Grandres. You are the master of your fate."

"I will remember we had this meeting," Grandres said. "As a system lord, you have always kept me informed, and I believe you will crown me with the Titan Crown as you promised. Now, I must attend to other matters."

"May the gods look down upon you and show you favour in these difficult times. I will inform Mocowas of our discussion. However, I must warn you that the Yatavra military will maintain a strong presence on Planet Daheza from now on. This is the way of the System Lords. Daheza, the largest planet for many light-years in all directions and home to the legendary gem canyons, is a favourite destination for many veteran System Lords. They granted you and the Reduzen race control of the planet because they desired beings with a rich history to inhabit the lands and develop into powerful civilisations that would prosper and benefit from each other's presence. It is a pity you are now at odds, but that planet will never be allowed to become a warzone. I will see you after the harvest festival. I wish I could attend. Next time, I will. Goodbye, Grandres."

Hetkarej turned and walked away, as did Grandres. Words were not wasted, and as the sensors ceased transmitting the holographic projections, Hetkarej pondered the unrecorded nature of their conversation. Grandres had made his intentions clear, and Hetkarej wanted the Kalicos king to have the advantage in everything.

Chapter Seventeen

Mocowas strolled through his heavily guarded estate on Hawtokax, the largest planet in the Keshiwen system. The security-conscious supreme lord master owned private estates and large luxury sea vessels for entertainment. The ocean creatures on Hawtokax were said to be mesmerising.

Stopping in front of a tank of jujowek fish, red and yellow with small blue dots on their tails, sharp teeth, and protruding black eyes, Mocowas tapped the tank. The fish went into a frenzy before calming down. Stepping back with a smile, he entered the adjoining holo-comm room, standing before his holographic sensors. A technician activated a console at his nod, and a holographic projection of Hetkarej materialised.

Hetkarej grinned and bowed slightly. "Hello, Supreme Lord Master Mocowas. I am glad to see you looking healthy and strong."

Mocowas responded with a forced smile. "The rumours of my imminent demise have been greatly exaggerated."

"I never credited those tales, Supreme Lord Master. I firmly believe in your enduring and purposeful reign. You excel in your role."

Mocowas, feeling satisfied, smirked. "Thank you, Hetkarej. I am confident you will serve the next supreme leader well. Let's discuss the pending war between the Kalicos empire and the war breeders."

Hetkarej appeared uneasy. "The second day of fighting above the planet has been devastating. Queen Fasjey has lost hundreds of fighter pilots, numerous cruiser fleets and two major carriers in systems protecting Queen Xunaseta's planets."

"This war will cost the Reduzen queen dearly, win or lose," Mocowas stated intently. "Queen Fasjey is preparing hundreds of thousands of warriors, anticipating a larger conflict. Her forces could number in the millions within a few cycles."

"Grandres is fully informed of her plans," Hetkarej interjected.

"That concern lies with you, Hetkarej, not me."

"What plans do you have post-war with the renegade force?"

"I aim to construct magnificent libraries on our homeworld and fortify our military further."

"And the new regime structure you've mentioned?"

"I intend to empower the citizens of Etrehen. A citizen gatekeeper will represent them, and I'll reduce the council of System Lords. We don't need so many overseeing the empire. More decision-making power will go to the System Lord, who succeeds me. I never sought to be perceived as the most powerful Supreme Lord."

Hetkarej, struggling to conceal his frustration, complimented, "You are truly a great leader." He privately lamented that Mocowas's decisions would make it impossible for his supporters on the council to challenge Esekal's future rulings, potentially diminishing his influence among the System Lords.

Mocowas stood calmly and declared, "Soon, I will dispatch the largest patrolling fleets of cruisers and carriers in Yatavra history. We will hunt down and eliminate every member of the renegade force. Our Attackers will be deployed to scour every area of space for potential targets. Following the war's conclusion, we will concentrate on regulating the Reduzen and the Kalicos. We will develop a master plan to address the challenges the Giyehe and several other races pose that threaten our supreme reign."

"We will dominate every alliance and become the ultimate challengers that can never be defeated. The day you command the fleets to begin their voyage will be remembered as a significant day, Supreme Lord Master."

"It is beneficial that we discussed these matters, Hetkarej. I must contemplate the structure of every forthcoming event, which could alter the course of history to the extent that we become the dominant race in any system known to all beings we encounter."

"Battles will be fought and won over time, but in the end, regardless of who wins or loses, they will all bow down to us."

"Yes, Hetkarej, they will."

Chapter Eighteen

Hundreds of cruisers and carriers approached Qukosi for one final battle between the Kalicos fleet and the Lutresas battle fleet protecting the planet. Heturadi planned to commence bombing the planet by the end of the fourth day of attacks, confident this could be achieved at every level. The bombing would last an entire day, with the ground battle starting at night on the planet. Heturadi knew Mewetesi's forces could regroup with the Reduzen fleet. Still, the intergalactic gladiators needed to begin their campaign on the planet's surface. He was there to safeguard the passenger shuttles carrying the gladiators and intended to use every means to protect Vatemfa's elite fighters.

Heturadi approached the communications operator's hub. "Send a message to all the ships involved in this final attack. We must adapt our plans based on the offensive tactics implemented by the enemy. Mewetesi is astute and will aim to weaken us with a defensive line if we all bombard the planet simultaneously. Now, the fleet commander engages us from afar. The Lutresas will fight with unprecedented ferocity."

A young female operator with a notably deep voice responded, "Your orders will be relayed, Fleet Commander Heturadi."

The pilot announced, "We are nearing the planet, Sir. I'm informed of considerable debris in space around the planet. The new coordinates provided will offer us a clearer path. We should anticipate attacks upon exiting hyper-light drive speed."

Another operator reported to Heturadi, "Sir, I've been informed that seventy per cent of the planet's defence systems are destroyed. The captains on-site report they're still under heavy fire. They recommend deploying as many cruisers as possible, with additional attackers required."

After a moment's thought, Heturadi decided, "Dispatch eighty-five cruisers ahead. Hundreds of our attackers from three separate fleets, summoned from two different systems, patrol the area, seeking the remainder of Mewetesi's fleet to eradicate them. Deploy half into battle and request reinforcements from the four systems where intergalactic gladiators await deployment. Instruct fleet captains to deploy a quarter of their attackers to search for the enemy in systems near the contested planets. We must eliminate every Lutresas adversary."

The operator began to execute the commands, "I will notify all relevant superiors of your instructions, sir."

Heturadi addressed the crew, "After our gladiators have devastated the lands, we'll deploy mega hypersonic bombs and lower the territorial cannon stations to our enemies' planets. This war may seem unending to our adversaries, but every strike we deliver will be decisive. Be prepared for anything. Do not disappoint me and pray to Siritusu, the ultimate conqueror and our deity, for our gladiators to triumph over the war breeders and their slayers."

As the ship's pilot remained motionless, focused on the navigational controls, Vatemfa appeared on the bridge, receiving salutes from the security crew. He watched the hyper-light waves flash, envisioning victory and dominance over their foes.

Vatemfa turned to Heturadi, "I see security is in place on the bridge as you ae about to make the final push in this battle against the enemy. What news do you have for me?"

"We will emerge from hyper-light drive speed shortly," Heturadi stated as he approached Vatemfa. "I've dispatched some ships ahead of us to clear more than one path. We must initiate the bombing of the planet once again after the gladiators have left it in ruins. Grandres desires for Queen Xunaseta's slayers to be slaughtered on the battlefield before our ship's bombs decimate everything she values. I have commanded attackers to seek and destroy all Lutresas fighters on sight."

"Soon, the almighty intergalactic gladiators will have their day," Vatemfa growled, his grin malevolent. "I want every civilian to tremble with fear as they witness the demise of their protectors in the most gruesome ways imaginable."

A communications operator swivelled in her chair to face Heturadi. "Sir, the Reduzen Star Ranger fighters have arrived in large numbers alongside many cruisers. I'm monitoring the communications. The Lutresas fleet has suffered significant losses, and the remaining planetary defences are nearly incapacitated." After briefly pausing, she continued, "New Lutresas fighters have emerged with a fleet of cruisers."

Vatemfa placed a hand on Heturadi's shoulder. "We can gain the upper hand."

The operator addressed both Kalicos leaders, "Our attackers have encountered the remainder of Fleet Commander Mewetesi's main fleet. The ensuing battle saw heavy losses on both sides due to missile fire from the Lutresas cruisers. Mewetesi withdrew from the Mojhanen system before reinforcements could arrive. Scout ships spotted the fleet near the Yewose nebula, not far from the Zatodex planetary system, once controlled by the clone barons. It's rumoured that there are new facilities for creating hybrids for the war breeders. Our fleets sent to that location were forced to retreat, but more are en route."

Heturadi sneered, "If we do not halt Mewetesi, she will return with a vast armada. Let's hope the fleets en route to the Zatodex system can accomplish what is necessary." He then instructed the pilot, "Get us as close to the planet as possible, then we'll conclude this space battle and deploy the gladiators aboard our carriers to the planet. The Lutresas race will witness carnage once the intergalactic gladiators unleash their fury."

The crew faced chaos on the view screen as the pilot disengaged the hyper-light drive speed. Debris struck the ship immediately, prompting the pilot to adjust the course using pre-set coordinates.

The Lutresas cruisers and fighters engaged Heturadi's ship, adopting a defensive stance. Heturadi's flagship downed numerous fighters as they approached. Star Ranger fighters seemed to emerge from hyper-light drive speed from every direction, skillfully dodging and returning fire. The vicinity of the planet was fraught with danger, motivating every pilot, whether Kalicos or Lutresas, to fight for survival.

Heturadi acknowledged the ongoing challenge of space warfare. Even if he succeeded in deploying every gladiator onto Qukosi, the combination of Mewetesi and the Reduzen fleet commander, Ujesal, remained a formidable threat. In their day, they were an enigma to any adversary. Yet, Heturadi felt prepared for the forthcoming skirmishes and battles in space, confident in his ability to manage any assault. He believed the Kalicos forces would ultimately dominate the planet despite potential uprisings.

Heturadi observed numerous Reduzen cruisers clashing head-on with Kalicos cruisers. The two formidable groups of ships unleashed continuous fire upon each other, with the Reduzen cruisers employing their laser rail cannons—long, wide, single-barrelled weapons designed for maximum damage to the enemy's vessels. Spinning around and firing from both ends, the plasma torpedo port attachments relentlessly launched, stripping metal from some ships' hulls and causing significant damage. Another squadron of Lutresas vessels surged at high impulse speeds towards Heturadi's ship, with sixty more galaxy cruisers advancing at similar speeds. They unleashed every cannon at their disposal against the Lutresas cruisers, with Heturadi's ship fording ahead, shielded by the Kalicos cruisers.

"Inform the carrier captains they can start emerging from hyper-light drive speed now, Heturadi told the communication operators. "We will jointly press the attack on the remainder of the enemy ships."

The operators immediately relayed the order through the communications systems, wasting no time.

Heturadi, scrutinising the view screen, recognised the futility of the enemy's defences against their onslaught. Vatemfa, partially enjoying the spectacle, clenched his fist and gritted his teeth with each enemy ship's destruction. He shared a frenzied look with Heturadi as another massive explosion resulted from a Lutresas carrier colliding with cruisers to Heturadi's ship's left. The pilot adeptly veered right, narrowly evading the explosion.

Vatemfa roared, "This epic battle will be etched in history. Pilot, steer us to the edge and back without failure," he said, turning to Heturadi.

"After decapitating Xunaseta, I'll return home for King Grandres's celebratory feast. He will herald us as heroes."

The ship's bridge battle chief reported, "Sir, the rest of the fleet has emerged from hyper-light drive speed, and our final attackers are arriving. They will encircle the main fleet as we advance."

"Excellent; now we turn our attention to the ground assault," Heturadi commanded. "Summon the gladiator carriers to Qukosi. Instruct my fleet's carrier captains to prepare the passenger shuttles. We'll deploy them to the surface shortly."

Attackers burst from hyper-light drive speed, as Heturadi concluded. They dove into the fray, targeting Star Ranger fighters amidst a vast close-combat battle near the crumbling space stations that once bolstered the planet's defences. Outnumbering the fighters three to one, the attackers leveraged their advantage while the fighters employed cunning tactics in dense areas to evade laser fire and missiles. Missiles often struck debris, causing further chaos. Kalicos attackers collided with large metal shards, causing explosions and damaging Reduzen vessels that managed to return fire.

"I want to conclude this!" Heturadi bellowed. "Charge full-on and confront any ship that blocks our path. Urge the attackers to intensify their assault. Relay this to every communications operator on every ship in the fleet."

In response to the command, the larger ships escalated their aggression, and the melee intensified, resembling a scavenger fighter dogfight. Star Ranger pilots exploited the chaos by mimicking renegade force tactics, flying perilously close to larger ships to dodge enemy fire. Missiles filled the void, with Reduzen pilots daringly heading towards them, swerving away at the last moment, hoping that foes would collide with the projectiles. The Kalicos were cautious, aiming to avoid adding to the missiles indiscriminately filling every direction. They did their utmost to dodge the laser fire from pursuing fighters.

The Kalicos cruisers unleashed every cannon at their disposal in all directions while the Reduzen concentrated on ships attempting to breach their defensive line, aiming to prevent gladiator carriers from nearing Qukosi as they arrived. The Kalicos carriers launched over a thousand more attackers, instantly turning space into a lethal playground.

Heturadi commanded, "Inform the carrier captains to cease releasing more attackers. Additional fighters may arrive over the coming days."

The attackers overwhelmed the Star Ranger fighters, and the Lutresas fighters near the planet barely managed to approach the battleground before hundreds of attackers repelled them, destroying them in space. They plummeted towards the planet's surface, resembling giant fireballs as metal detached from the ships upon entering Qukosi's atmosphere.

"The victory is ours, Heturadi," Vatemfa exclaimed.

Heturadi grinned. "Deploy the first wave of passenger shuttles. Now, we'll see how the Lutresas warriors fare on the ground against the Kalicos' conquerors. Vatemfa's elite fighters will hunt like true predators. Wars are remembered longer when legendary foes are vanquished. This battle will be our ultimate test. I intend to dismantle the enemy piece by piece before returning home to Deheza; mark my words."

Chapter Nineteen

One hundred Sand cruisers adorned with designs representing Daheza's gem canyons passed by as Grandres stood on his balcony watching the parade. He was pleased to see his citizens enjoying the harvest festival, and news from Vatemfa that the intergalactic gladiators were on Qukosi soil bolstered his confidence in an imminent victory despite the anticipated losses.

Valeskin smiled at the sight of food stalls decorated with cream and aqua-coloured flowers floating above the ground, offering the sweetest fruits and largest vegetables selected by the garden servants of Loyanz. Eager for the feast, Valeskin looked forward to indulging in abundant meat and stewed fish, followed by various flavoured cold syrups drizzled over his favourite desserts.

The parade grew louder as gladiator guard trainees marched past, the first row of two hundred and seventy guards blowing loud horns and wielding laser spears crafted by the planet's arms masters. Renowned for their skill, these specialists create the finest weapons. The trainees donned brown barukath skin, appearing silk-like yet as durable as leather. Barukath, eleven-foot beasts native to the desert, journey to the jungles to find solace in their final days under the shade of trees. Both the Kalicos and Reduzen nations treasure this symbolism, utilizing the skin for clothing. The trainees' black boots, adorned with small gold spikes on the soles, symbolize their sole purpose to protect the king and his palace. Four hundred and fifty guards marched past King Grandres, saluting by extending their fists to the side, placing their hands on their hearts and bowing. Grandres smiled and waved, then rested in his silver and white chair.

Next, the royal court's elite servants of Bretasi caught Grandres's attention, dressed in black togas secured by bronze pins adorned with rubies from the Elatrian mines. Their faces, concealed behind white Kalicos ghost masks with painted red tears, signify their solemn duty to prepare royal families for death and attend to their immediate needs in dark times. Positioned above all other servants, these elite servants are selected from specific bloodlines, a tradition spanning thousands of cycles.

Grandres's excitement peaked with the appearance of arms masters displaying ancient weapons once wielded by great kings. The sight of spears and swords that vanquished formidable foes over many cycles was awe-inspiring. Dressed in green and beige uniforms resembling loose bodysuits, the arms masters bore cycle dates on their sleeves, marking eras of Kalicos military victories.

Rising to salute the arms masters, Grandres received a reciprocal gesture. Valeskin followed suit, earning the same respect from the veteran weapon experts. The Kalicos citizens cheered and waved enthusiastically, their voices amplifying the parade's energy as it wound through the capital. The gladiator guards' horns contributed to the din that filled Loyanz.

Reflecting on the war's potential outcomes, Grandres felt the weight of his years. Recognizing the need to fortify each planet under Xunaseta's control and increase military presence, he contemplated the strategic concessions he might offer to Mocowas, seeking to gain an advantage without compromising his authority. A master strategist, Grandres was committed to enhancing his empire's military capabilities through the efforts of his engineers and arms masters. Anticipating a war of unprecedented scale, Grandres's ambition to emerge as a legendary figure, revered above all leaders, remained undiminished.

The parade continued along the mud-ridden roads of the city. Sacred horn blowers, stationed in temples to play after each prayer service before the festival, briskly marched past. Tall Kalicos males, towering over 6'5", donned red and green uniforms with reflective slacks and tops accented by a black sash over their shoulders. As they moved, their instruments, shaped somewhat like large sea shells and elongated at both ends, were directed sideways towards Grandres and Valeskin, emitting long, powerful blasts that resonated above the crowd's din.

Grandres watched as the procession neared its conclusion—smoke billowed from steam kitchens and huts, signalling the impending feast to celebrate the festival. Citizens joyously tossed white powder and black ash into the air, honouring the life and death of mothers who bore workers gathering the harvest. This harvest, presented to the Yatavra, not only sustained the citizens of the Kalicos empire but also financed a military growing stronger across many systems. The food not consumed by Yatavra citizens would be sold to nations that were allies of the empire. Grandres and Valeskin stood and saluted, then retreated into the vast armoury from the balcony. This led to a study housing a library of rare books recounting tales of ancient tribes from the old Kalicos homeworld, Zetrax. As they traversed one of the palace's largest wings, reflecting on their race's history and its future, they were saluted by gladiator guards stationed along a gold-and-white painted corridor. Despite Grandres feeling the fatigue of age, he remained confident in his continued reign and the prospect of rejuvenation after rest.

Awaiting them in the food hall were the council of the royal court and elite members of the Kalicos nation, gathered for one of the cycle's most significant celebrations. Descending grand marble stairs with a silver balustrade, they noticed small sparkling desert stones embedded along the edges. The foyer, flanked by gladiator guards, signalled the harvest festival's tradition of showcasing guards throughout the palace.

Approaching the food hall, visible through tall double doors, they observed tables laden with fare from across Bretasi and beyond stews, meats, fish, broths, vegetables, salads, sweet desserts, fruits, and various sweet and alcoholic beverages. Servants stood ready behind each chair, with others at the hall's rear holding pitchers for the imminent feast.

As Grandres and Valeskin entered, the guests applauded. Seating themselves, Grandres summoned his servant, "Serve me some meat stew to fill my gut and accompany it with some wine," he said, patting his belly and yawning. "My son will have the same."

After serving their stew, the feast commenced, with guests either directing servants to their preferred dishes or serving themselves.

Emwefi sat beside the king, speaking between mouthfuls of salty seaweed, "Your Majesty, the war we are currently engaged in will have significant repercussions. Xunaseta's allies are contemplating retaliation. They are considering supporting the Reduzen queen and her fleets as they combat ours."

With an arrogant smile, the king replied, "I don't believe we have anything to worry about. The Yatavra-System Lords have clarified that should the war escalate, they will deploy their military forces to prevent a full-scale intergalactic conflict. Any race inciting the wrath of Mocowas would face severe consequences. His focus remains on the renegades, nothing more."

Having finished his seaweed, Emwefi served himself some fish stew. "Mocowas will continue his battle against the renegades until none remain. On the ground, our gladiators will ferociously eliminate any Lutresas warriors posing a threat. The upcoming three days are critical; we must gain the upper hand."

Anfeku, seated next to Valeskin, carved generous portions of roasted Reweska sea serpent for himself, coupled with boiled vegetables and freshly squeezed fruit juice. After consuming half a goblet of juice, he addressed Valeskin while biting into a serpent tailpiece, "Prince of Daheza, you've been in daily contact with Vatemfa since the war's onset. What insights have you gained?"

Pausing his nectar consumption, Valeskin shared, "I've had extensive discussions with the general. He recognizes the necessity of securing not only the capital but also the smaller cities from enemy threats. Despite being only the second day of combat, the Lutresas have attempted to encircle our gladiators. We are preparing to deploy the second wave, led by the Blood Legion. However, we face significant challenges from Lutresas warriors on the city outskirts, who form large packs and predominantly strike at night. Our forces suffered considerable losses on the first night despite daytime advancements."

Reflecting on their longstanding friendship and Valeskin's growth, Anfeku envisioned him as a formidable, potentially more ruthless king than his father, "We have the opportunity to accomplish what the clone barons could not. Already engaged on Qukosi's battlefields against Xunaseta's elite, we face a gruelling challenge but must persevere. Our eventual triumph will silence the Queen of the Slayers' allies."

Valeskin, filled with vengeance, mused, "It would be most satisfying to see the queen's head adorning a gladiator's breastplate spike." His anger stemmed from the considerable losses inflicted on Heturadi's fleet and the intergalactic gladiators' slowed progress due to Qukosi's unforgiving terrains outside the cities.

Grandres, tearing into a grilled vetacav leg, ate with gusto, "Xunaseta's downfall is inevitable. War looms over this planet as Yatavra forces increasingly establish their presence to control Kalicos and Reduzen factions. Yet, the looming conflict on Daheza seems unavoidable. The Yatavra's current preoccupation with renegades presents us with an opportunity. If not this war, another will arise. I have shared this with my council, confident in its inevitability."

As the feast continued, those council members yet to speak were lost in contemplation, united in their desire for Grandres's supreme rule. Their loyalty was unwavering, and they were committed to victory at all costs, much to Grandres's satisfaction.

Chapter Twenty

Srankat, the head of the female guard and the Queen's personal protector, issued commands before Fasjey entered the room. The formidable warrior was concerned that the Queen would notice the distraction permeating among all who served her caused by the ongoing war news. As she barked orders, spit flew from Srankat's mouth, demanding her guards to stand at attention. She expected them to be prepared for anything, as the Yatavra military forces on the planet had been cordoning off the borders, isolating the land beyond the Panonetes territories. More than one enemy was on the planet.

The heavy-set guard rushed through the back entrance to the flower garden from the palace's second wing. Upon arriving, she spotted Ruyey, the Queen's secretive male confidant, friends with Swelok and Yelesu, her top advisor and the most influential female in the royal court besides herself. They made their way across the garden path towards the central flower beds, where several seats and two tables were arranged, one occupied by Fasjey.

Fasjey greeted her two friends and trusted royal court members, confident in their collective capabilities. Despite the war's toll on her people, she deemed it necessary, willing to commit various acts to ensure survival if victory eluded her, even if it meant waging war against the Yatavra-System Lord council. Fearless, Fasjey was ready to push boundaries.

Srankat approached Fasjey as Ruyey and Yelesu greeted the Queen. Fasjey motioned towards the wooden chairs beside her, inviting the council members to sit. Ruyey, known for his stubbornness, arrogance, and brute strength, took the seat to Fasjey's left. Yelesu, comparatively small for a Reduzen female, sat opposite the Queen.

As Srankat moved closer, hoping to overhear the Queen's discussion on the war after her report, she stood at attention before the ruler who governed lands spanning half the planet.

Fasjey queried, "I presume my female guards are ready for war?"

Srankat responded promptly, "Yes, Your Highness. The Queen's guard recognises your authority and pledges to fight with honour until death. Guards are stationed at every palace corner, and as your guard, I request to remain by your side day and night, permitting only those I approve to substitute during my rest."

Fasjey, speaking kindly, assured, "On palace grounds, I feel secure with the current arrangements, Srankat. However, to ease your concerns, remain here with me until lunch. Afterwards, I'll retire to my chambers before the afternoon's council session."

Srankat, accepting the directive, positioned herself to the Queen's side, her muscles evident, hand resting on her laser gun, perfectly still.

Fasjey, amidst the fragrance of her garden, envisioned a future of unbounded rule, free from wars that threatened to engulf her nation in a perpetual conflict waged by beast warriors.

The dark Queen turned to Yelesu and shared, "I have received word from Ujesal. The fleets have regrouped at the Zetodek system, and there are numerous reasons I believe this was the correct decision, much like the fleet master himself. However, I also want him to seize every opportunity to attack immediately. We can now not prevent the ships above Qukosi from dispatching passenger shuttles filled with intergalactic gladiators to the surface. Thousands are landing daily. We are now committed to defending Xunaseta's additional interests."

Yelesu stood up, slightly fidgeting, "I hope you don't mind, Your Highness. I prefer to stand when I feel anxious."

"I've observed this about you recently," Fasjey noted, avoiding over-analysis. "Share your thoughts with me."

Straightening her posture, Yelesu cleared her throat, "We must adapt, which is precisely what Ujesal, our fleet commander, excels at. He should intensify attacks on Kalicos ships delivering supplies to Qukosi. Additionally, our Star Ranger fighters and the hunter cruisers must be proactive, with clear directives to obliterate all gladiator carriers well before they reach their destinations."

Fasjey, visibly agitated yet concerned, responded, "This strategy means deploying our ships close to Qukosi for continuous assaults, risking significant losses. The involvement of the Giyehe, who have been tirelessly constructing ships for us, could escalate if King Grandres perceives a threat. I must alert Prime Architect Dekrehas that war might soon arrive at his doorstep."

Ruyey, increasingly perturbed, raised his voice, "I didn't attain my stature without paranoia about our cunning and deceitful adversaries.

Grandres should leverage his powerful allies with substantial military capabilities to confront the Giyehe. These allies, situated near Kretaq, the supposedly impenetrable Giyehe homeworld, will face a true test. This conflict could prolong significantly as more parties become involved."

Fasjey acknowledged, "Your insights mirror my own concerning our future challenges, Ruyey. This battle will be our toughest yet. Familiarity with suffering may become inevitable, but we must persevere for our freedom. Upon Oshdan's return from Tribaj, we will assess our ground force capabilities with Jarkepe here and on other planets."

Yelesu revealed, "Our breeding programs for combat beasts continue unabated. The training grounds on undisclosed planets remain our best-guarded secret. Yet, Mocowas and his lords know we're amassing an unparalleled ground force. Jarkepe reports that one million combatants will be ready within a cycle, with an additional half a million shortly after that. Spread across thirteen planets, our four million fully trained warriors remain hidden, poised to become an unstoppable force and our revered legends."

Fasjey, with a grin, expressed optimism, "We've always been well-prepared for battle, ensuring sufficient provisions for all my subjects, from labourers to warriors."

Yelesu added confidently, "Though Mocowas anticipates challenges, he won't foresee our approach. He expects confrontation sooner rather than later."

Fasjey's resolve hardened, "We will be prepared for anything Mocowas or any other adversary can muster. Jarkepe and our Reduzen strategists specialize in countering opposition, ensuring the expansion of my realms. Rest assured, we will not falter in achieving our ultimate ambitions, leading with a ferocity that our allies and the gods themselves will acknowledge as we triumph over those daring to oppose us in battle and beyond.

Chapter Twenty-One

Intergalactic gladiators sprinted through a small forest, crossing a field towards some bushes two hundred metres beyond the last trees, with Zasadus, Qukosi's largest city, under attack in their sight. The Kalicos territorial cannon stations, significant in size, bombarded the city. In contrast, the Lutresas' defensive laser cannons targeted the enemy weapons, causing dramatic explosions upon their destruction, which could be heard two cities away. Lutresas warriors, bracing for a formidable battle, were recovering from the initial onslaught that had tested their front lines. Within the city limits, patrols combated attacks from above as citizens faced the chaos of their homes being targeted.

Armed with dark green and black laser guns and long daggers featuring a gold line down the blade and a black and purple handle, the gladiators' metallic armour was adorned with spikes. Their arm and leg armour was comparatively thinner, complemented by thick black boots and brown gloves. Each gladiator was equipped with spare weapons – two daggers at their belts' back and a laser gun on the right thigh, alongside six high-intensity pulse grenades on a left-side belt clip.

Four additional battalions approached Zasadus from various directions, signifying the onset of a significant challenge as more gladiators arrived in shuttles. Determined to weaken the Lutresas slayers' resolve, the gladiators' numbers increased by the minute. Lutresas commanders Ukuratan and Fosdrusi countered this threat by deploying their warriors in larger groups and spreading out to intercept the arriving gladiators.

Upon reaching the city, the gladiators faced stiff resistance, with the confrontation turning exceedingly violent. They dispersed as Lutresas warriors unleashed laser fire, impacting seventy gladiators directly. Despite injuries, many gladiators persisted, driven by their resolve. The Lutresas warriors, clad in black and white battle suits with metallic chest and belly armour and some wielding shoulder launchers, launched missiles to disrupt the advancing gladiators.

As missiles rained down, gladiators were propelled in all directions. Yet, many rose faces set with determination, continuing their advance as comrades' limbs scattered around them. Responding with laser fire and grenades, they ensured each throw was impactful. The Lutresas warriors sought cover behind sky cruisers, these long, oval-shaped grey and blue vessels equipped with rectangular landing gear, crafted from a metallic alloy, extending when the landing was necessitated.

Sky cruisers, designed for higher flight than converted sand cruisers, soared above the dark grey stone roads of the city square, now marred with large holes and dents from various explosions. The gladiators, advancing towards the warriors, aimed their laser guns at the warriors' legs. As they fell, some warriors managed to target the gladiators, aiming for the head and hitting their mark more often than not, a skill ingrained from a young age. Unbeknownst to the advancing gladiators, hunters had been summoned, arriving on sky cruisers, launching overhead attacks and dropping armed missiles on them. The battle, involving the tallest and strongest Kalicos fighters, intensified as four hundred gladiators reached the city square, met by two hundred slayers on sky carriers.

As the sky cruisers landed, launching missiles into the crowd of gladiators, the fighters dispersed to engage various groups of warriors, many of whom were already struggling to rise. The gladiators formed circles, firing outwardly, as additional forces joined from the city square's side entrance, near a monument building with a domed top and spires. Hunters, arriving on converted sand cruisers, contributed to the blue and red laser fire crisscrossing the square as bodies fell en masse.

As the gladiator ranks thinned, they were replenished, with territorial cannon stations joining the fray. Pulse grenades launched towards the tall warriors caused chaos while other Lutresas hunters advanced, firing their long laser guns, penetrating the gladiators' chest armour with repeated shots. Close combat ensued as the gladiators engaged with daggers and hand-to-hand tactics.

The territorial cannon stations indiscriminately attacked, sparing only those recognized as Kalicos gladiators by their AI systems, although some gladiators were caught in the crossfire. As the battle raged, warriors and gladiators sought cover, the cannon stations moving erratically, targeting the renowned slayer army.

Despite the gladiators' intent to encircle the warriors, their plan was doomed. Battalion leaders adapted, dividing their forces to mirror the hunters, intensifying their assault on the city's defenders. As the battle escalated, territorial laser cannons supported the incoming gladiators. At the same time, sky cruisers were targeted by grenades, causing significant destruction. The city's cannon defences retaliated against the territorial cannon stations, causing widespread damage.

Despite the intensity of the combat, the gladiators pressed forward, overwhelming the slayers with their sheer numbers and the additional support from space whilst throwing grenades into slayers who were bunched together as they approached their targets. The Lutresas army, bred for war, resisted fiercely, demonstrating their indomitable spirit. As more territorial cannon stations arrived, spreading chaos, the gladiators continued their push, supported by territorial missile stations. The city, under General Vatemfa's orders, faced the prospect of total devastation, a grim testament to the brutal conflict engulfing Qukosi.

The Blood Legion gladiators, in a swift second wave, encircled the city just as missile stations arrived, launching projectiles at the city's defensive cannons. This strategic delay in the arrival of missile stations was to clear surrounding areas and support the passenger shuttles, delivering the Blood Legion and the other gladiators. The battle against the Kalicos fleet ships in space was intensely contested, with patrols targeting gladiator carriers long before they could deploy their shuttles amidst the debris. Moreover, Blood Legion gladiators targeted not only the largest city but also the second and third largest cities of Qukosi, confronting formidable defences and the Gazaxa beasts, yet to face the might of the Blood Legions.

The Blood Legion's uniforms distinguished them with longer spikes on their shoulder plates and helmets adorned with golden-tipped spikes made from the hardened skulls of jawanga beasts, resembling large, horned gorillas. Renowned for their unwillingness to accept defeat, the Blood Legion relished the prospect of challenging the legendary Slayer army.

As thousands of warriors and Gazaxa beasts were en route to reinforce the city, the missile stations inflicted substantial damage, impacting monuments dear to the citizens of Qukosi. The ground trembled with each explosion, igniting flames that engulfed nearby beings. Occasionally, cannon stations caught in these blasts plummeted, causing casualties among both armies.

Unleashing their mega laser guns, the Blood Legion, numbering four thousand in each Legion, engaged hundreds of Lutresas slayers in the square, swiftly cutting them down. Despite some tall warriors managing to launch missiles, causing minimal damage, the Legion's advance was relentless. Missiles launched by Lutresas warriors often backfired, adding to the chaos and carnage in the square.

Splitting into smaller groups, the Blood Legion pursued hunter packs to decimate as many slayers as possible. Supported from above by cannon and missile stations, they strategically cleared paths and targeted defensive cannons. Sky carriers, arriving to join the fray, provided crucial cover fire and targeted the city's artillery defences, marking the beginning of widespread destruction on the third day of fighting.

As endless waves of gladiators flooded the city, the slayers bravely countered at every opportunity. Armoured passenger cruisers, escorted by a convoy of sky carriers, made landings on the city's outskirts, prompting missile stations to attack, aiming to decimate both the arriving forces and the Gazaxa beasts.

Top Lutresas slayers, utilizing portable hovering laser cannons, delivered devastating wide bursts of laser fire against the gladiators. Despite attempts to retaliate with mega laser guns and grenades, the gladiators suffered severe burns, with some grenades detonating prematurely, causing additional injuries. The slayers, pressing their advantage, ensured no gladiator survived the onslaught, showcasing the brutal intensity of the conflict that escalated with each passing day.

The slayers aimed their cannons skyward, targeting territorial laser stations that had bypassed the city square, moving towards the city centre to assist the gladiators in their offensive. The Lutresas warriors successfully shot down these laser cannon stations, causing them to crash into buildings, erupting into fireballs of red and white sparks before plummeting to the ground below.

In the forest, explosions resounded as sky cruisers provided cover for the passenger cruisers ferrying the Gazaxa beasts, shielding them from the missile stations that targeted any movement on the ground. Emerging from the forest, the Gazaxa beasts, donned in their customary light armour, which helps them adapt to the weight of their shoulder cannons to maintain agility for close combat, advanced towards the city. With the pilots and warriors manning the weapons controls effectively and hundreds more passenger cruisers en route, the battle for the city was far from concluded.

Three hundred beasts swiftly covered the ground, aware of the Blood Legion gladiators preparing for this pivotal historical moment. They aimed to capture Qukosi from the slayers and their Queen, defeating the esteemed warriors of their archenemy. Continuous deliveries of territorial cannon and missile stations descended from the carriers above, with Heturadi and Vatemfa intent on inflicting maximal destruction, envisioning the eradication of every standing city to leave the citizens without refuge, his ruthlessness mirroring that of Grandres and his council.

As the beasts approached the city's edge, numerous gladiators emerged to confront them, unleashing repeated laser fire aimed precisely at the gladiators' heads, causing devastating injuries. The gladiators targeted by the initial shots were either killed instantly or struck in the beasts' less-protected lower torsos. Though some beasts fell and struggled to rise, they continued to fire at passing gladiators until they were overwhelmed by enemy fire from ground forces and aerial laser stations.

As the Gazaxa beasts adopted a quadruped stance, they leapt towards the gladiators, who prepared their defence by kneeling and firing their laser guns. In a tactical formation, some gladiators formed circles, while others positioned themselves on the flanks, all firing in unison. Despite multiple hits, numerous beasts closed in, slashing the gladiators' faces with their claws, removing chunks of skin, and even biting into them while continuing to shoot, creating a chaotic battleground. Despite sustaining headshots and falling lifelessly, the ranks of the beasts were continually replenished by thousands more storming in from the woods, undeterred by the explosions that propelled them around, quickly regaining their footing to charge anew with ruthless efficiency.

Meanwhile, Lutresas warriors, alongside Gazaxa beasts, navigated the forest's perilous terrain, the air filled with laser fire. Gladiators attempting to confront the emerging Gazaxa from the forest were met with precise fire. Using trees for cover, the warriors repelled attacks from all directions, even as sky cruisers above unleashed lasers and missiles, leading to sporadic explosions. The downing of sky cruisers by territorial missile stations added to the chaos, resulting in significant casualties among both gladiators and warriors. However, Lutresas warriors, resilient in the face of adversity, managed to eliminate many gladiators upon regaining their stance, with Gazaxa beasts savagely attacking any remaining adversaries, ensuring a gruesome scene of carnage and destruction.

With thousands of Gazaxa beasts deployed to defend the city against an incessant influx of gladiators delivered by Kalicos carriers, Vatemfa and his captains remained unwavering, confident in their eventual victory. As Gazaxa beasts, with unmatched ferocity, advanced towards the city, the battlefield witnessed brutal confrontations, with gladiators falling victim to their own weapons and the lethal strategies of beast warriors and Lutresas slayers alike.

The battlefield, strewn with casualties from both sides, illustrated the sheer intensity of the conflict. Gazaxa beasts, drenched in blood, relentlessly pursued the gladiators, employing laser fire and physical might to overpower their foes. Despite the gladiators' attempts to retaliate, targeting the beasts' legs and faces, the overwhelming force and tactical prowess of the Gazaxa and Lutresas warriors proved formidable. The battle, marked by fierce engagements and strategic eliminations, showcased the determination of the defenders to safeguard their city against the encroaching threat, embodying the relentless spirit and unwavering courage that defined the essence of their struggle.

As gladiators converged from various directions, it appeared the warriors were at risk of being outflanked, with territorial weapons stations hovering ominously above. Utilizing portable cannons secreted within city structures, the Lutresas warriors launched a counterattack from the city's rear, targeting the gladiators' lower torsos. The Blood Legion, caught off-guard, dispersed to confront the Gazaxa beasts, their separation rendering them more vulnerable. Despite the beasts' formidable leaps and attempts to engage, the gladiators swiftly retaliated with their mega laser guns, pre-empting any potential harm from the beasts and inflicting severe burns through their armour, leaving many dead or dying.

Amid this chaos, laser stations targeted the fallen beasts just as additional sky cruisers entered the fray, promptly destroying the laser stations. Missile stations retaliated against these cruisers, igniting a fierce aerial battle that resulted in sky cruisers being downed, their crashes causing massive explosions and high casualties among the gladiators. Surviving slayers and beasts took this opportunity to eliminate any incapacitated foes nearby. Other cruisers persisted in assaulting the remaining Blood Legion gladiators, prompting a brutal ground engagement where no quarter was given. Utilizing daggers and laser guns, the combatants inflicted grievous wounds, with Gazaxa beasts employing their natural weapons to devastating effect.

Despite their valiant efforts, the slayers observed their numbers diminishing, aware of the continued arrival of Gazaxa reinforcements amidst relentless waves of gladiators. Fatigue began to set in among the Lutresas and Reduzen forces. Yet, the battlefield, littered with the fallen, spurred them to persist, driven by the belief that victory remained within reach if they fought with unity and resolve. This indomitable spirit typified the warriors' ethos. Yet, the meticulous strategy deployed by Vatemfa's ground forces had inflicted considerable damage, casting doubt on the defenders' capacity to withstand such onslaughts. Grandres's anticipated satisfaction with the outcome underscored the gravity of their situation, compelling Fasjey to prepare her forces for the inevitable counteroffensive.

Tshekedi Wallace

Chapter Twenty-Two

⸻◆⸻

The Giyehe delegation was deeply engrossed in discussions about the daunting aspects of the ongoing war, with Dekrehas meticulously examining the conflict details through a holographic viewscreen. Despite the dire statistics, Dekrehas was not taken aback, knowing well the formidable nature of the races embroiled in the conflict. Queen Fasjey's prior warning about the looming war highlighted Grandres's resolve to challenge any provocations, a stance further complicated by the robust alliance between the Giyehe race and the Reduzen empire.

Wesyal, the esteemed general of the Giyehe army, voiced an urgent call for readiness, aligning with Paltovis's decision to gear up for a significant clash. Their determination was palpable: securing victory was imperative to prevent Mocowas from seizing what remained. Dekrehas echoed this sentiment, stressing the need for caution and ensuring their allies were well-prepared.

Wesyal, known for his commanding aura, underscored the vital need for relentless combat, advocating for open communication with allies about the imminent threats. The arrival of Razcet, Dekrehas's brother-in-law, sparked further dialogue on the fate of their race amid rising tensions. Despite the mounting pressure, Dekrehas remained composed, encouraging Razcet to express his concerns.

Razcet, acknowledging the bleak situation in Qukosi and the overwhelming losses incurred, sought Wesyal's insights on Paltovis's defensive tactics. Wesyal elaborated on their strategic stance, emphasizing the fleet's role in safeguarding nearby and distant territories alongside ongoing efforts to bolster Fasjey's forces. Given their broader territorial reach compared to Queen Xunaseta, reliance on Reduzen support was deemed crucial. Mocowas's aspiration to dominate Fasjey appeared momentarily hindered. Yet, her potential relocation might spark a more formidable military resurgence, attracting wider support.

Razcet voiced his confidence in their defensive capabilities against Grandres, cautioning, however, against underestimating the cunning and paranoia of the System Lords, highlighting the grave stakes involved.

Dekrehas then signalled attention. "Let us not lose sight of the formidable challenge we may face. However, his resolve will be tested by the renegades distracting Mocowas and leaders contemplating distancing themselves from him for greater autonomy. Our immediate focus remains on addressing the current threat efficiently. Wesyal, with numerous fleets stationed in space, I suggest to Paltovis that, while we must avoid overextension, we should aim to assert our influence further afield in less powerful regions. Fortifying our position and forging new alliances will be crucial."

Wesyal acknowledged the strategy, revealing plans to leverage Queen Fasjey's connections in systems where her Gazaxa beasts are bred as starting points for establishing strongholds. This symbolized the unity and collective resilience of the Giyehe and Reduzen races. Katseu, the pioneering labour chief, observed the discussion. Her trailblazing role in empire reconstruction set a precedent for how empires could be reshaped through the efforts of dedicated labourers. Katseu, with her elegant demeanour and an appearance that exuded a sense of refined grace, turned towards Wesyal, adjusting her visor-like dark glasses that shielded her eyes from the glaring sunlight filtering through the windows of the prime architect's tower.

The Giyehe delegation engaged in earnest discussions, with Katseu expressing concern over the populace's reaction to the impending war, stressing the importance of maintaining public order. Dekrehas acknowledged her point but prioritized the warfare strategy, understanding the significance of public sentiment yet focusing on the broader conflict.

Katseu underscored the expectation of Wesyal's leadership in formulating battle plans and ensuring the defence of their cities, to which Dekrehas, gazing out the window, pondered the systemic challenges faced by the System Lords and the potential opportunities for renegades to exploit any perceived weakness in Mocowas's reign.

Razcet envisioned the downfall of the Yatavra empire as a momentous occasion, with Giyehe cruisers playing a pivotal role in dismantling the oppressive regime, foreseeing a time when the sun over Etrehen witnesses the surrender of armies to the combined forces of Reduzen and Giyehe.

Dekrehas, activating a sensor, mused on the inevitable losses from the forthcoming intergalactic conflict, urging resilience and reflection on

Xunaseta's plight, with Wesyal revealing her attempted escape thwarted by Heturadi's forces. He lamented the occupation of Qukosi by Grandres, noting Vatemfa's challenges in maintaining control and the leadership transition to Alpha Guardian Boprexu.

Katseu offered her support for the reconstruction efforts post-conflict, with Dekrehas affirming the commitment to aid allies through adversity and proposing an envoy to demonstrate solidarity with Boprexu. As Wesyal excused himself to continue his military duties, Dekrehas concluded the session, emphasizing the importance of diligence and the determination to prevail in the conflict, signalling a readiness to confront Grandres and assert their autonomy in shaping their destiny.

Departing the meeting, Dekrehas, accompanied by Razcet and Katseu, approached the exit, utilizing his identification badge for access, embodying the resilience and collaborative spirit of the Giyehe leadership in the face of impending challenges.

A computerised voice resonated from the tiny speakers above the door, prompting, "Prime Architect Dekrehas, enter." Dekrehas, accompanied by his colleagues, entered his library, excited about the discussion away from General Wesyal. Surrounded by shelves laden with historical tomes detailing the Giyehe's interstellar conflicts, they contemplated the impending challenges of war.

Dekrehas, reflecting on a past intergalactic conflict that spanned eleven cycles and resulted in significant losses before the Yatavra seized the opportunity, underscored the resilience of many races despite the devastation. Razcet, recalling their formidable defences that Supreme Lord Master Valazon and the royal family of Etrehen couldn't breach, highlighted the Giyehe's enduring strength.

Katseu, amidst these reflections, voiced her concerns over the grim aspects of their history, recognizing the sacrifices made for their empire's autonomy. Dekrehas emphasized the necessity of strategic innovation to outmanoeuvre adversaries like Grandres, known for his cunning distractions.

Razcet proposed intensifying their defensive strategies across all governed planets, underlining the ongoing expansion and exploration efforts as vital to their advancement. Dekrehas, feeling the weight of his responsibilities, acknowledged the daunting challenges posed by Vatemfa and Heturadi, determined to persevere in their objectives despite the opposition.

A moment of solemnity ensued as Razcet expressed unwavering support for Dekrehas's leadership, foreseeing a time when the architect would join the revered record keepers in Sekasdar, watched over by the gods. He envisioned a resolution to their tribulations, asserting that adversaries would eventually succumb.

Concluding the discussion, Dekrehas, marked by a grave demeanour, reflected on the inevitable sacrifices required for freedom, underscoring the unacceptable notion of defeat. The group resolved to assess their foes carefully, aware that any misstep would bear significant consequences, reaffirming their commitment to overcoming any challenge.

Chapter Twenty-Three

The industrial cities on planet Rasodorn, home to the enigmatic Otrizon clone barons, were alive with activity. High above, Admiral Buculaz's space force maintained a vigilant orbit under the discerning gaze of Mocowas, who took pleasure in his blend of exotic fruit wines. Amid his galaxy-wide inspections and tactical deployments, thoughts of the ceasefire at Trebaj that may never last and the imminent threat posed by Grandres's recently unveiled mega cruiser flagship, the Goliath, preoccupied him. Grandres's eagerness for conflict with the Giyehe and Reduzen races was unmistakable, driven by territorial setbacks on Trebaj and a burning ambition to further cement his supremacy.

As Mocowas pondered these developments, he was joined by Head Baron Tirehesa, the formidable leader of the Otrizon, and Baron

Vinektel, a distinguished member of the clone barons renowned for his affluence and the pioneering cities he established. Their presence in the soaring city of Rasodorn signalled a momentous assembly, eclipsed only by the towering security of the Pewedrev dynasty's citadels, a stronghold within the metropolis.

Feyesma Pewedrev, the chief scientist and a beacon of cunning and intellect, entered the scene, carrying a legacy of groundbreaking innovation and a palpable sense of fatigue from the unending cycles of conflict that plagued the clone barons. Tirehesa, embodying the physical prowess of the Otrizon, initiated the meeting, keen to delve into the repercussions of Xunaseta's downfall and its ramifications for the clone barons.

Mocowas, asserting his authority, declared that with Grandres's consolidation of power on Qukosi, the planet would fall under the dominion of the System Lords Council, safeguarded by the Otrizon clone guards. This pronouncement was a critical juncture, heralding a strategic alliance and a shared vision for the future.

Vinektel audaciously voiced a grim desire for Xunaseta's end. Mocowas acknowledged this with a pragmatic recognition that her demise, by any means, represented a significant triumph. Tirehesa expressed regret over the abruptness of her termination, unveiling a collective yearning for a more prolonged retribution.

The discussion then turned to Fleet Commander Mewetesi and the Reduzen queen's reinforcement of her ranks, highlighting the tenacity and resolve of their foes. Tirehesa's affirmation of readiness to face Fasjey and her allies underscored the clone barons' determination and the complex network of alliances and rivalries that shape the cosmic political terrain.

Mocowas, teetering on the edge of exasperation, instead declared with conviction, "I will adopt stringent measures against Fasjey. She has caused me sufficient grief, and it's time she faced the repercussions. I anticipate she will double the food and precious stones contributions from the last cycle. Moreover, she will incur a tax threefold the previous amount in Zelcres credits as part of our strategy to bolster our fleet and eliminate renegade elements. I am aware her allies might come to her aid should I initiate the attack, yet I remain undeterred. My System Lords are always prepared to rectify and penalize those who dare oppose us."

Feyesma, actively participating in the dialogue, leaned towards a bowl of dried fruits and reflected, "We must be ready for any offensive. I will direct my proteges and their teams to craft the most exceptional cloned guards. Xunaseta's governance over a hidden army of warriors presents a covert danger; they might unite and incite unrest. We must neutralize them promptly to avert any rebellion that could challenge our hegemony."

After indulging in another sip of wine, Mocowas set his cup down, focusing on the forthcoming strategy, "I plan to execute bombings on selected regions of the planet as soon as the Kalicos intergalactic gladiators retreat. This will dissuade the citizens of Lutresas from entertaining any notions of insurrection."

Baron Vinektel, surveying the array of fruit and wine with a lack of interest, soon voiced his expectations, "Mocowas, your realm ensures the collapse of those who dare challenge the empire you have established. Nevertheless, it is imperative that we swiftly quash any defiance against our edicts." Clad in his favoured purple and blue robes, adorned with gems and diamond-encrusted rings, he signalled to an attendant, "Bring us a selection of meats and the most exquisite nectar at hand. My craving for sustenance and libation is considerable." Upon his command, the servant-initiated a round of applause, and a procession of others arrived, bearing an assortment of meats to the table. Further attendants emerged, presenting pitchers of sweet nectar and wine before exiting. Vinektel then poured himself a generous glass of nectar.

"I aspire for us to ascend once again as a dominant force," he declared, his plump fingers clasping the goblet, nearly salivating at the taste of the sweet nectar. "With each new dawn, I envision the formidable forces we shall muster for you, Mocowas, and the prospects you will thus afford us. My anticipation grows for our expansion deeper into the cosmos and the conquest of new domains."

Mocowas, smiling, reassured him, "You shall have the territory and all else you have sought. Our dedication lies in backing such a pivotal ally, one in harmony with the vision of the Yatavra-System Lords Council."

"I value your readiness to bolster our expansion, Mocowas. This alliance promises to bring mutual benefits to our people. The clone barons harbour a profound grasp of supreme entities from bygone eras. Future generations of Otrizon barons will establish myriad dynasties fortified by our partnership. This auspicious event calls for celebration."

As Baron Vinektel relished his nectar, Mocowas encouraged all barons to indulge in wine. United, they toasted and partook in the beverage, commemorating a future that, for now, appeared promising. However, Mocowas remained cognizant of the persistent menace of the renegades and resolved to confront them when necessary. This task was complicated as the renegades had disappeared after safeguarding their newly claimed planetary system against the Borshux miners. For the time being, they remained elusive, leaving Mocowas to navigate the subsequent demanding phase of his governance.

Chapter Twenty-Four

Grandres surveyed the sea of Daheza before his gaze shifted to Valeskin, who energetically engaged with hundreds of gladiators on the beach. This stretch of sand, extending from the palace grounds, was reserved exclusively for Grandres and his royal lineage. In the distance, Grandres's fleet of convertible flying cruisers sailed, recognisable by their rectangular form and spherical ends that housed the propulsion systems. These vessels, relatively tall and wide, were designed to accommodate a modest crew primarily for security purposes, in addition to the bridge personnel and a few servants.

Princess Cerewey, distinguished by her slightly fuller facial features yet possessing a healthier and taller stature than many Kalicos women, sat beside Grandres. Clothed in a fine pink and black silk dress with a white satin cloak that danced in the wind, she contemplated the future cities that symbolised the alliance between the Yatavra and Kalicos military forces. Amidst this contemplation, news arrived from Hetkarej that Fasjey had clandestinely departed Daheza, refusing further tax contributions to Mocowas.

Valeskin signalled to Grandres, "The palace abandoned by Queen Fasjey could serve as a command centre for our military elite to make critical decisions. Fasjey's mining operations, now on Kalicos territory, will enrich us further. As a queen without a realm, reclaiming her losses will prove difficult for her."

Grandres, irritated by Fasjey's actions, thought, "Fasjey's escape complicates matters significantly. Her unforeseen departure, along with many ships, has left me frustrated. The oversight by the System Lords has jeopardized my mission to eliminate a threat."

Valeskin, moving away from his guards and escorts—who fulfilled the dual roles of security and personal aides to the royal family—joined the discussion.

Cerewey rose, approached Grandres, and assured him, "Your Majesty, I am confident in your ability to realise your ambitions. You are a formidable force; with the right strategy, no adversary can withstand your military might."

Grandres, looking out towards the sea, declared, "Many dawns may pass before I finally seize the opportunity to confront Queen Fasjey. However, I will instruct the Hecaja and Vatemfa to target their allies if necessary and meticulously plan to acquire as much territory as possible. This will lay the groundwork for establishing a grand empire."

Together, the trio walked along the beach, the future on their minds as waves gently lapped at the shore.

"Father, your strategic prowess will undoubtedly make Mocowas recognise you as one of the greatest kings. The people of Kalicos will celebrate you as their hero. Esteemed leaders will respect you, while the less formidable will fear your reign. The Supreme Lord Master may have employed similar tactics. Still, our military will prove superior in effectiveness and efficiency, growing stronger as the conflict escalates."

Grandres responded with a malevolent chuckle, proud of Valeskin's potential as a future supreme ruler, destined to cast a long shadow from which only the most adept successors could emerge.

Cerewey, the wind picking up, adjusted her cloak's hood, "We must tread cautiously as we engage in warfare. While we aim to outmanoeuvre and ultimately surpass the System Lords, keeping Mocowas informed of our intentions is vital. We foster an illusion of consideration for his perspective by consistently seeking counsel. We must manipulate his perceptions and sow discord among the System Lords and their allies, regardless of their stance towards Mocowas's rule."

Valeskin smiled at his wife, "By anticipating Mocowas's moves and demonstrating loyalty, including offering our fleet's support against his adversaries, we will cement our position as his stalwart ally. Then, Hetkarej will undoubtedly bestow the Titan Crown upon my father."

Grandres pondered momentarily before stating, "Upon receiving the Titan Crown from Hetkarej, I will arrange for a discreet coronation. The flagship Goliath will be readied for battle, marking the onset of our campaign against our adversaries. This era will be historical, for we will emerge as rulers of a new kind, heralding the dawn of the titan empire."

Chapter Twenty-Five

~~~~~~~~~~~~~~~~

Ikizuni surveyed the desolate expanses of Wukundel, hands poised on his hips, confronting the barrenness that persisted despite the absence of environmental toxins. Resolute, he recognized the renegade force's declaration of war against Mocowas's empire, readying for a campaign aimed at inflicting severe damage and signalling unwavering determination.

Elevated to the pinnacle of command over the conglomerate of pirate and scavenger fleets, Ikizuni embraced his role, fostering a culture of fearlessness and ruthlessness among his ranks. He envisioned a strategy of stealth and surprise, planning to establish hidden bases on the inhospitable planets of Wukundel and Heraskal, leveraging their desolation as cover. His tactics involved dispersing a fraction of his fleet for surgical strikes against Yatavra's strategic outposts to dismantle the infrastructure crucial to their military and research endeavours.

Departing Wukundel aboard a passenger carrier, Ikizuni pondered the sacrifices and challenges ahead, acknowledging the inevitable losses yet driven by a predator's instinct. His forces, swelling daily, prepared for relentless engagement. At the same time, he remained aware of the potential coalition of foes, including the formidable Otrizon clone barons, known for their relentless assault tactics mirroring those of the renegades.

Upon his return to the Ravage, Commander Letroxi, a paragon of multi-domain combat, greeted him. Letroxi's respect among the fleet as the successor to Ikizuni underscored the unity and dedication of their forces. After dismissing the weary pilot to recuperate, Letroxi and Ikizuni proceeded, steps in unison, toward the shuttle shafts, ready to strategize for the imminent confrontations.

Ikizuni boarded the shuttle, awaiting them and said, "We will be up against it in the Pusdek system. The research facilities are top-secret, but Mocowas knows that the traders can be bought, so there will be hundreds of attackers and many cruisers in the area."

"This was inevitable, my friend," Letroxi replied. "It was always going to happen, and nothing is ever easy. We will lose friends and great warriors. We are aiming to obliterate a top target. Once this job is done, Mocowas will divide his fleet even more, and we will be in a better position overall."

Ikizuni took a moment to think. "Bridge," he said into the shuttle's intercom. "I just want to harm our enemies in every way we can and win this war. Then we can do as we please and live in peace."

"We are a long way from achieving that. Once we meet with Mewetesi and see where Queen Fasjey stands in this, we will better understand how to proceed with the next part of our battle plan. Fasjey is difficult to read, but she is ready to attack the System Lords on many different fronts. As an ally of Xunaseta, she would be angered that Qukosi is under the control of her sworn enemies. We will capitalise as when her warrior beasts fight; they do so knowing their queen wants the enemy to die a nasty, brutal death."

Letroxi had grey-brown eyes. The almighty commander was musclebound with a strong brow. The Rotumze genius had dark brown skin and grey hair speckled with white. His humanoid body was tall, and his arms were hard-skinned with a bone structure that was among the most solid of any race. His long reach was perfect for hand-to-hand combat. His strength during battle in the past was unrivalled.

The shuttle shaft reached the bridge, and the two fleet commanders stepped onto the most significant deck of the ship. Ikizuni absorbed the vista of Heraskal, his thoughts dedicated to safeguarding all those who depended on him for guidance and had never doubted his leadership. A sense of foreboding in his gut forewarned him of the perilous journey ahead—a journey from which he might not return whole, if at all. Yet, he had resolved to stand firm, unwavering in adversity. He harboured the hope that others shared his resolve, whether they fought for causes akin to his warriors' or sought vengeance for past injustices. Should the Yatavra and their allies fall, it would affirm the possibility of victory and freedom for the renegade forces. This singular aspiration drove him, though he recognized that the path to liberation would be fraught with battles and the war would be prolonged and arduous.

The future remained uncertain, and like many before him, Ikizuni's fate was yet to be determined. He had always known that every soul, perceiving something at stake, would eventually need to choose a side and confront the ensuing trials. This belief was Ikizuni's creed; he was prepared to live or perish by the sword, ensuring his impact was felt. The ultimate conflict loomed on the horizon, an unstoppable force heralding the war to end all wars.

Chapter Twenty-Six

Fleet Commander Paltovis shifted on a lengthy seat on the bridge of the Giyehe moon cruiser flagship as they neared the Zatodex system. Seeing Mewetesi's ship on his viewscreen sent a wave of apprehension through him, aware of the impending war that could potentially shatter him. Despite standing at a modest 5'8", Paltovis's broad, masculine torso exuded positivity and confidence. His energy was palpable, complemented by his rare sky-blue eyes—a distinctive trait among the Giyehe. His skin bore a rugged texture around his beard yet remained smooth across his face, adorned with a small, inconsequential mole above his right eyebrow.

The moon cruiser was an imposing vessel featuring dual bridges and main observation decks, resembling a half-globe atop a horizontally pointed rectangular base. Its sides bristled with laser cannons and interspersed missile ports, with additional armaments crowning the half-globe. The ship's dark green and red livery bore the Giyehe black flag and the silver firebird of Kretaq, depicted spewing golden flames—a nod to ancient tales of firebirds capable of fiery breath, though the real creatures merely irritated with their spit. These legends faded with the Giyehe's emergence from isolation. The emblematic Giyehe flag adorned each moon cruiser and the accompanying carriers. Paltovis was resolute in engaging any Kalicos ship they encountered, pledging allegiance to the Prime Architect Dekrehas's call to arms.

The ship's tactical strategist, Derogoxal, entered the bridge, querying, "Sir, Mewetesi's shuttle is nearing. Shall I escort him to the war room upon his arrival?"

Turning with a smile, Paltovis responded, "Yes. I'll wait for him there to discuss our plans."

"I eagerly anticipate your strategies, sir," Derogoxal remarked before departing for the docking bay.

Rising, Paltovis addressed his crew, "Halt the ship immediately. I'm off to hear Mewetesi's account. Her clash with the invading Kalicos fleet was fierce. Standing on the cusp of conflict with the Yatavra, we must brace our crews for the formidable challenge ahead. I leave the bridge to you now. Captain Baklaza, ensure I'm informed of any developments in the ongoing skirmishes between the Kalicos and Reduzen close-combat vessels."

Baklaza, a loud, seemingly unwelcoming Giyehe battle specialist, replied robustly, "Yes, Fleet Commander Paltovis. There has been no chatter on the communication link yet. However, I will contact you through your communication as soon as any information comes in." Paltovis then walked off the bridge onto a short diagonal gangway and stepped into the shuttle waiting in the shaft to his left.

Immediately, Paltovis called out, "Ship's War Room." The shuttle sped down the shaft and stopped on the arms gallery deck where the war room was located. As the doors opened, Paltovis disembarked and entered the war room through an open double door. He sat down at a desk featuring holographic sensors embedded in the table, which illuminated in red on a black background—a design favoured by Giyehe engineers.

Paltovis was a war tactician of exceptional skill. He was known for his ability to outmanoeuvre the enemy with menacing prowess unmatched by his peers. As a young fleet commander, he had faced formidable opponents, including evil warlords, in numerous battles and wars. While he never shied away from confrontation, strategic retreats were part of his captain's experience. His primary concern was choosing his battles wisely in the impending war, acknowledging that he couldn't always assist those who fought by his side in his younger days. Important battles elsewhere meant that assistance could not always be extended to those in need. Paltovis was acutely aware of the strategic decisions required of a fleet commander, often determining the targets for his ships' attacks.

As Mewetesi and Derogoxal arrived, they sat opposite Paltovis. Though fatigue was evident, Mewetesi expressed her gratitude for the meeting. "I am grateful that we are meeting, and I thank the gods for allowing me to be alive," she said.

Paltovis, placing his hand on his heart and bowing his head, expressed his respect, "Fleet Commander Yosuntuk, you are alive because you are a formidable space combat strategist. The gods fashioned you to be one of the finest. I hold you in great esteem."

Derogoxal echoed the sentiment, bowing his head and touching his chest, "I recognize the sacrifices made in leaving your home. I am committed to fighting alongside you to protect the remaining Lutresas-owned planets. Alpha Guardian Boprexu now leads the Lutresas race. Together, we will elevate him to prominence before Mocowas and his nefarious forces can exploit vulnerabilities."

Paltovis smiled confidently, "With our gods' favour, we will not falter. I sense it. Once the Giyehe resolves to take a stand, all who oppose us will regret their actions, facing a force divinely blessed and driven by sheer passion. The end will see the Yatavra-System Lords defeated by legendary warriors, celebrated eternally by leaders and citizens alike. We are committed to seeing this through, eradicating an evil power. This will be our legacy, spoken of for generations."

Mewetesi, moved yet composed, added, "Your support is unforgettable. This moment marks the onset of an oppressive regime's downfall. We are on the cusp of making history. Let's start by addressing the newly constructed military space stations in unmonitored systems. While our close combat vessels should patrol our regions, ensuring no sector is overlooked, each patrol must comprise no fewer than five vessels."

Paltovis stroked his beard, nodding thoughtfully. "You're correct, I believe. Our patrols have been spread too thinly, as we've aimed to move covertly to avoid drawing undue attention. Our planets, shipyards, border patrol bases, and space stations are under close surveillance. The Yatavra deploy their patrol ships to restrict our movements. Dekrehas has informed me that with the dawn on Kretaq tomorrow, we will be at war with the Yatavra-System Lords. This must surprise Mocowas, who perceives our movements merely as a demonstration of strength while he fortifies his own. The absence of the renegade commanders from this meeting, due to their oversight of assaults on key space stations and research facilities, underscores our commitment. We shall unite with the renegades in a strike on the Yatavra space station orbiting Akovatek, and the military installations on the planet's surface will not be spared—they are to be bombed and obliterated. With the Reduzen lending their cruisers and the combined might of fighters from Giyehe carriers and renegade ships, we will be well-equipped to defend ourselves and assail the formidable Yatavra military strongholds."

Mewetesi expressed her concurrence with the strategy. "This will serve as an impactful opening salvo. The System Lords know they are targets for overthrow yet remain oblivious to the origin and focus of the impending assault. Only utter annihilation will suffice. The renegade fleets are already coordinating with Redezun and Lutresas strategists and commanders from other allied forces to ensure our strategies are aligned. We must stand united in the face of Mocowas's inevitable counterattack, which promises to be as formidable as our initial strike, if not more so. His disregard for the civilians of any nation on the planets he targets at his most ruthless is well documented."

Derogoxal, drawing from his wealth of experience, added, "Mocowas will aim to eradicate the fleet of any aggressor and their allies, potentially in a single decisive blow or through a dual-front assault. He will seek to confront our unified fleets directly, striving to decimate many allied fleets' military bases and spaceports. They will be compelled to respond should he make such a move."

Paltovis took a deep breath, their situation settling upon him. "So, here we are, on the brink. Truly, we're nearing the point of no return, with none of us pausing to contemplate the reality that we are outnumbered in many respects unless the new fleets we desperately need can be prepared swiftly."

Derogoxal rose, his gaze sweeping over the war room with laser guns, ancient maps, and quotes from Giyehe philosophers inscribed on the walls. "We have less than a quarter of a cycle to construct the ships and the new space stations, which will serve as ports for repairs," he stated. "That's why the assault on the space stations orbiting Akovatek is critical. With hundreds of ships in the region, it will be a true test of our might and ensure considerable damage is inflicted. The chaos we create will undoubtedly leave the Yatavra-System Lord Council in disarray, leaving them uncertain of our next move. Over the coming five days, we will determine our immediate targets, executing strikes as we proceed. Our strategists, constantly moving in their ships and shielded by a formidable convoy, will adapt new tactics daily."

Mewetesi, with a note of optimism in her voice, shared, "I am genuinely hopeful about our chances of victory. The Lutresas scientists produce thousands of clones in the Zatodek system factories. With your support, we are set to expand our facilities across three additional planets. By the end of the next cycle, we'll have an innumerable force of pilots and ground troops trained to engage in combat at an exceptionally advanced level."

Chapter Twenty-Seven

One hundred renegade fighter ships penetrated enemy territory, poised for an onslaught. They identified a Yatavra space station in the distance, alongside several unattended close-combat Yatavra vessels. The Jekaxtu fighters discharged their missiles towards the station and the docked ships. The resultant explosions were monumental, startling the station's crew awaiting passenger shuttles for transit to cruisers and carriers elsewhere. As crew members hustled to the observation rooms in response, the fighters directed their laser fire at the base, triggering a colossal blast that punctured the staff quarters' fortified sections. Crew members were ejected into the void of space. Subsequently, the fighters aimed missiles at the docking port, its obliteration dispersing debris into the observation rooms and causing bodies floating in space to be cleaved by jagged metal shards.

The fighters, piloting with adept precision, circumnavigated the base. An additional seventy fighters converged on the scene, employing their hyperlight drives to join the fray from a distant system. The attack was meticulously orchestrated, with the arrival of the ships precisely timed. Among them were Rotumze close-combat fighters and their Jekaxtu renegade counterparts, battle-ready, their pilots exuding confidence and expertise.

The sizable military space station behind the Yatavra base rallied its forces. As several groups entered just as the Rotumze and Jekaxtu decelerated from hyper-light speed, the situation became dire for them. A squadron of six dozen Yatavra attackers advanced towards the renegade fighters. Despite their smaller size, the Yatavra missiles delivered a formidable impact.

The Yatavra attackers charged at the fighters, intending to dissect the one hundred vessels and obliterate as many as possible. Their strategy was nearly successful. With astonishing velocity, they unleashed a barrage of laser fire. The renegade pilots adeptly dodged most of the onslaught, pre-empting the manoeuvre. Aware of the ferocity of the Yatavra assault, they understood the peril of delayed reactions. As additional Jekaxtu fighters materialized from hyper-light speed and stationed themselves, picking off numerous Yatavra assailants idling in space, the Rotumze ships executed continuous rotations about their axis with their propulsion systems, launching attacks from various angles. At the same time, the attackers futilely attempted to surround them.

The military station's formidable laser cannons, comparable in size to smaller passenger carriers, unleashed their full firepower. Missiles from the fighters and cruisers hit them in critical areas. Despite sustaining partial damage, the cannons kept firing. The cruisers intensified their assault, aiming missiles at every laser cannon on the military station. The observation areas, armoury galleries, and security team quarters were struck on all levels. Subsequently, the cruisers focused on the staff sleeping quarters and the main engineer's level, causing devastating damage.

The military station seemed to be engulfed in flames, with debris causing further destruction. Hundreds of Yatavra fighters, summoned after the space station commander requested aid from the nearest planetary military base, emerged from hyper-light speed, bypassing the system where the battle raged.

The attacking pilots, driven by animosity towards their adversaries, pressed on. Fighters from another system were en route, but for the time being, the Jekaxtu and Rotumze ships maintained a defensive position, repelling as many attackers as they could.

Some fighters arranged themselves in two lines, with the first line engaging the enemy and the second turning. Hence, their rears faced each other, firing at approaching ships from various directions. The remainder of the fighters engaged in a fierce dogfight with the attackers, striving to distract them and prevent them from penetrating the two lines between the military installation and the base station.

Navigating around the debris proved challenging for the attackers due to their ships' length, whereas the more compact Rotumze fighters easily manoeuvred through tight spaces. The renegade vessels, rotating on their axis, shot the attackers occasionally. Skilled pilots would dart past debris with enemy ships in pursuit, shoot the debris, and then sharply turn as the resulting collision turned the attackers into flaming wrecks and twisted metal.

As more fighters joined the fray, the battle descended into chaos, with attackers dispersing in attempts to inflict maximal damage on the renegades. The cruisers fired indiscriminately while fifty fighters targeted the research facility with missiles. Two large groups of attackers pursued them, firing relentlessly as explosions ravaged the research facility. However, they arrived too late. The space station shifted off-axis, tilting vertically as its systems malfunctioned and onboard flammable chemicals detonated, exacerbated by debris and laser impacts.

The attackers, pursuing distant fighters fleeing the station, were caught off guard by a relentless missile barrage from behind. The Yatavra ships managed to eliminate several pilots who had attacked the research facility, rendering the close-combat vessels ahead inoperative. Yet, the victory was short-lived as the renegade pilots met swift ends.

The renegade captain, commanding the operation from a Rotumze cruiser, ordered a retreat. Every ship activated its hyperlight drive engines, fleeing the embattled sector. Although many fighters escaped, some were left adrift; their pilots were engulfed in fear as they faced encirclement and attack. These forsaken warriors would be hailed as heroes by their comrades. The cruisers withdrew, and their targets were annihilated, scattering debris. Some larger ship fragments remained, with pilots cast into the void, their expressions empty in the face of war's unforgiving nature.

Nothing would halt these campaigns until the renegades achieved true freedom and the Yatavra-System Lord's military was no longer a threat.

Chapter Twenty-Eight

Servants and guards assembled in King Loheyal's second residence, which was repurposed as the meeting venue for the Yatavra System Lords, known as the Golden Monument of Etrehen. The palace's exterior gleamed with gold, and its pillars were a fusion of gold, marble, and stone. Statues of silver and gold adorned the palace grounds. At the same time, the bronze and metal fountain at the garden's heart featured a golden depiction of the planet's yellow fruit trees, a testament to both beauty and craftsmanship. This palace had stood for sixty-five cycles.

Mocowas and Esekal, followed by Pakowe—a man of short stature with a face that bore the marks of weariness, darkness, and moodiness—entered the room, the walls of which bore the flags of conquered nations. Mocowas was prepared to deliver a speech, after which he might permit his two grand lord masters to contribute, should it be necessary. Among the council, only these three held the privilege of being prioritized speakers during the war, a status Mocowas had tirelessly cultivated. His obsession with maintaining absolute control was unyielding.

Only half the council was present to hear Mocowas speak. Other System Lords had been assigned to various planets to supervise the established political frameworks and ensure strict adherence to orders. On Etrehen, Gorxab had once been charged with subjugating the citizens. Mocowas, leveraging his family's renown for pomp and circumstance, was adored by the planet's inhabitants. Now, more resolved than ever to remain on Etrehen unless compelled otherwise, Mocowas governed with an iron fist, having reassigned Gorxab. In Mocowas's absence, Pakowe was entrusted with a fleet command from the flagship.

Mocowas noticed Tarukev, a young and ambitious military leader with his own formidable fleet, positioned at the room's rear. Tarukev, known for his lethal prowess as a ground force commander, would not hesitate to commit acts of violence for Mocowas if it promised advancement. Mocowas, having previously mentioned to Esekal that Tarukev might have risen to the supreme lord in another era, kept a vigilant eye on him. Although that opportunity had elapsed and Tarukev lacked the key attributes of a top Yatavra System Lord, Mocowas believed that, under the right circumstances, Tarukev could still be hailed as a legend in his era.

Seated on a long brown and black chair, flanked by his two most trusted lords, Mocowas felt the drugs, administered twenty-four days ago following the initial attack, exert their effects, fortifying his muscles and tripling his heart's strength. Traditionally, such drugs were reserved for System Lords of his age during wartime, intended for short-term use with intervals and a strict diet—a contrast to the young planet guards and

Yatavra army troops who could endure them for extended periods cycle after cycle.

The assaults on space stations and research facilities had begun to undermine Mocowas's military dominance in space. Reduzen and the newly constructed Lutresas ships had targeted Kalicos and Yatavra vessels in groups. This situation compelled Mocowas to ally with the Kalicos King, inadvertently playing into the King's strategy. The Kalicos fleet had experienced exponential growth. In dire need of every ally available, as more races joined the renegades each day, the Supreme Lord was cognizant that even emperors were reportedly siding with the opposition. It seemed inevitable that more imperial forces would declare their support for the rebellion, spurred by rumours of Fasjey's interactions with empresses who had long admired her and endorsed her cause.

The Mortarsa homeworld and other planets under the control of these master builders had been subjected to relentless bombardment, prompting Pakowe to deploy countless fleets for their protection. This necessity frustrated him, as he aimed to maintain a formidable presence across vast regions of space. He considered the Kalicos king and his adherents opportunistic yet recognized their potential for genuine loyalty to the System Lords, especially if rewarded for their contributions to a victorious campaign. The Mortarsa, as one of the Yatavra's staunchest allies, had surpassed all expectations, overshadowing the Kalicos race's contributions, which had long irked Mocowas. Equally adept as the reclusive Cetilsun race, the Mortarsa were already planning new cities on Yatavra planets they had wrested from races intimidated by their might.

Clearing his throat, Mocowas commanded a male servant, "Bring me some water, pup, and make haste. I abhor waiting." The servant promptly exited and returned with a water goblet, presenting it to Mocowas, who drank eagerly.

"Take this," Mocowas directed after finishing the water. "You and the other servants may depart now." The servant collected the goblet and left with the others. The guards then spread out as additional heavily armed protectors entered, ensuring the System Lord was never without protection in these tumultuous times.

Mocowas's speech bore the distinctive Etrehen accent—articulate, with a husky, deep, robust tone and a slight croak at the end of each sentence. A deliberate pause followed each sentence's conclusion, and the initial word of the subsequent sentence was drawn out—a characteristic Yatavra speech pattern.

"I want all of you to understand that the recent attacks are not merely among the worst we've faced. The Lutresas and Giyehe are demolishing so many space stations that we've been forced to decommission others. However, they wouldn't dare target our stronger planets, giving us ample opportunity to orchestrate a significant offensive against Giyehe and the remaining Lutresas worlds. We will eventually uncover the renegades' clandestine bases. The Reduzen queen, Fasjey, and her general have vanished. Sixty per cent of the populace under her reign have evacuated the planet or sought refuge in the vast desert cave system, a region neither the Kalicos nor we dare to explore. The creatures inhabiting the caves will likely be their downfall. We will consign the remaining Reduzen citizens to lifelong toil in the mines. Rest assured, we will capture Fasjey, subject her to public humiliation, and then execute her before she can consolidate further power. Pakowe will brief you on the next steps for our fleets."

Pakowe, speaking confidently, declared, "We possess more than enough ships to contend with the current dilemma. Countless attackers have been neutralized, and Reduzen cruisers have decimated some of our older cruisers and carriers. Yet, our principal planets remain under stringent protection. I foresee no civilian casualties, and our military personnel stationed on planets with bases will remain unscathed. Nonetheless, we must instil terror; thus, I've directed our ships to target known associates who have previously supplied arms to the renegade factions. They must be reminded of our formidable presence. I'm convinced this strategy is our best course of action. The collateral damage will undoubtedly be high, but the targets are warmongers and so-called freedom fighters, whom their people mistakenly venerate as prophets with divine connections. These individuals, disseminating Ikizuni's propaganda and those of his ilk, along with their domiciles, must be obliterated and erased from memory. They will be voiceless by dawn, their existence extinguished, and their advocates silenced."

Esekal, rising to her feet, proclaimed, "Soon, we will eliminate our most formidable adversaries, and after that, our singular aim will be total domination." She initiated a round of applause, and the other System Lords joined in, all eyes in the room converging on Mocowas. He was a figure consumed by malice, malevolence, and an ambition to etch his name in the annals of history. He saw himself as a beacon of resistance against an insurmountable foe, a conviction he believed time would vindicate, regardless of the renegade forces' resilience.

Chapter Twenty-Nine

———✧———

Eighty-five Gazaxa warrior beasts encircled Fasjey and Jarkepe as the two Reduzen legends engaged in conversation. Fasjey, admiring the beasts, offered a warm smile. The dignified queen then cast a serious look at Jarkepe, acknowledging the peril faced by the citizens she had left behind on Daheza. They all recognized that their ruler had to champion their cause. Fasjey had decided to lead her military from planet Roquexel, ensuring her safety from imminent threats.

Jarkepe addressed his queen, "Your Highness, by the end of this cycle, we will have one million Gazaxa beasts prepared for battle, with additional forces being readied shortly. We are progressing ahead of schedule. I've learned that every leader, previously thinking they had another cycle to bolster their ranks, has expedited their troops' training for earlier readiness. Moreover, the Mortarsa builders, backed financially by several races, including the Borshux, are gearing up to construct as rapidly as the Giyehe. Mocowas has enticed them with the promise of shared governance over the cities they develop, with both races' militaries safeguarding the Mortarsa's handiwork."

Fasjey responded with composure, "All of this was to be expected. A response of this nature was inevitable. The Giyehe are formidable opponents, and the System Lords are desperate not to be bested in future confrontations. Yet, I am certain they will be. I've heard whispers that even the most secluded emperors and empresses are eager to meet with us, offering support with supplies and arms for the upcoming battles. They detect Yatavra's weakness and are keen to witness the end of their expansive dominion."

Jarkepe, with a grin, remarked, "The inaugural ground force assault will be our litmus test. Following our setbacks on planet Qukosi, our beast master is hungry for victories."

"Our forces on planet Qukosi were vastly outnumbered by the intergalactic gladiators dispatched there," Fasjey observed, momentarily unused as she headed towards the Gazaxa beasts' training grounds. "Such was the influx of gladiators that the largest cities on the planet succumbed by the third day's end. We've covertly assembled many warriors, forming a force our foes are unlikely to surpass."

Oshdan moved through the high brown grass of the training fields, designed to emulate the terrain of Yatavra-controlled planets, where citizens dwell in uniform environments. The military installations, prime targets, utilized the tall grass for hiding defensive weaponry and camouflaged personnel. Bowing to his queen, Oshdan greeted Jarkepe with a warm smile—a rare gesture—and expressed immediate respect.

"Our esteemed general remains as serene as he was incensed before the tempest. Tempering your rage against formidable adversaries is challenging, but your anger doesn't dominate you. We must avoid negligence at all costs, for uncontrolled tempers lead to recklessness," Oshdan advised.

Jarkepe almost chuckled, "Oshdan, enlighten me with your strategy, my friend. I'd prefer that to be reflected on my temperament by you."

Oshdan's demeanour shifted, "Were we to seize any territories our renegade allies believed they could swiftly invade and plunder before consulting our strategists on currently viable targets, we'd gain a substantial advantage. We ought to reevaluate their approach, and I have one million five hundred thousand troops ready for an immediate offensive. We aim to wreak havoc and spare none at the System Lords' numerous military training camps. What are your thoughts, Jarkepe?"

Jarkepe reflected briefly before offering some insight to the beast master. "I plan to target the military installations as the renegades have suggested. I needed your confirmation on the feasibility of such an operation. We can bomb the Yatavra on planets where they conceal their secrets and conduct their manufacturing. Their factories would be decimated, and a significant number of troops and guards would perish. However, the true turning point will come when our warriors, with their bare hands, eliminate thousands of the enemy. This will radically alter the war's dynamics, revealing their true capabilities over a short span. Then, we will be poised to launch continuous strikes once we gauge their response."

Fasjey then expressed her insights, drawing from her vast experience, "Based on what we know, we can predict how the System Lords might react. Tales of their demonic essence are well-documented. It wouldn't be surprising for Mocowas to emulate the Yatavra supreme lords of old, such as Nesrodrel. Tomorrow, I shall convene with the Hecazy, Rotumze, Noxret, and Jekaxtu renegades to determine which allies will principally safeguard the freedom-fighting nations that lack adequate protection. While we cannot shield everyone, our priority must be to relocate as many vital individuals to our cause as possible."

Oshdan said, "Ancient military rulers from various races have stepped out from the shadows. Factions of freedom fighters and splinter groups are rallying, answering the call to arms. This is a development Ikizuni foresaw and welcomed."

Jarkepe continued, "Ikizuni has informed me that over one hundred thousand ships will bolster our current fleets. He's impressed but has mentioned the need for upgrades. The Giyehe will face a significant challenge. Empress Cesukrex of the Varsolak race has reached out to Prime Architect Dekrehas, indicating that while her fleets and ground forces aren't ready for full deployment, her engineers and financial resources will be at our disposal. Cesukrex's fleet commander has assured Paltovis of their readiness to fully integrate into our unified force within a quarter of a cycle. My eagerness for victory in this war has never been stronger. Every strike against the System Lords will vindicate any leader against tyranny. I have never feared death and am willing to make the ultimate sacrifice, taking others if necessary. We must embrace our destiny and fate, whatever it may entail."

Chapter Thirty

The Giyehe military space station and city in the Locask system were marvels. Ships frequently ventured here to witness the grand Jekosi nebula, a sight many captains believed would bestow fortune upon them. Despite this belief tracing back aeons, the tales of those legends who deemed the Jekosi nebula a blessing continue to be shared by great leaders.

Named after the system it inhabits, the city mirrored other military cities constructed by the Giyehe, taking the shape of a vast pyramid in space. Transparent in many areas, it was adorned with large silver, black, and gold metallic plating, covering specific sections of the nearly invulnerable glass-like screening. This allowed passing ships a peek into the expansive city. At the pyramid's base, docking ports buzzed with activity, connecting to the military space station—a long bridge-like structure equipped with numerous cannons and engineering rigs for repairs and rearmament.

Within Locask city, broad white pathways sprawled where inhabitants traversed, and dark grey shuttle shafts crisscrossed the structure vertically and horizontally, akin to a railway at the city's apex, reserved for the elite to convene and deliberate. Designated sections housed security and governmental departments, marked by a dark blue colour code, while green indicated agricultural departments for food production and distribution. While most space cities boasted similar security systems, the Giyehe excelled in fortifying their military-dominated structures. Carriers and cruisers amassed around the space city, complemented by two nearby military spaceports and a strategically located space station hosting thousands of fighters patrolling the Locask system continuously, maintaining constant communication with the city's hub.

Probes monitored the city's exterior and interior, scanning for environmental anomalies. Giyehe carriers, characterized by their long horizontal bridges with pyramid-shaped fronts and sterns featuring two horizontal wings, received probe reports. These carriers then relayed pertinent information to relevant city departments.

Despite the absence of visible cannons and missiles, the city harboured a vast missile arsenal ready for launch from peak ports. Retractable double-barrelled cannons, positioned halfway up and surrounding the structure, stood ready for immediate activation. Penetrating the city's defences, protected by numerous carriers and cruisers, would require a formidable attack, a fact widely acknowledged. The Giyehe had crafted an impressive city safeguarded with diligence.

Alpha Guardian Boprexu, stationed in the military base command centre, pondered his race's future amid support from various national leaders aiming to enhance the Lutresas' strength beyond precedent. These leaders sought to redefine the Lutresas' identity beyond their homeworld's fate. However, Boprexu detected a faction among the rulers aspiring to influence the politics and culture of their new homeworld. Mocowas had deployed fleets to safeguard interests he viewed as partly his own in Lutresas-influenced systems following the Kalicos invasion. The clone barons, seizing the opportunity presented by their adversaries' defeat and neglecting their treaty, now relied on their cloned army for security. The planet, practically divided between intergalactic gladiators and cloned troops, faced shared resource management under a tax to the System Lords. The clone barons aimed for full planetary control by the next cycle's end. Boprexu, aware of Grandres's solitary ambitions, recognized the king's cunning, suggesting his potential influence in the war could surpass any System Lord due to his relentless demand for power, supported by strategic advisors. Grandres's lineage, seasoned in conquest and survival, epitomized their enduring legacy.

Boprexu took a few moments to collect himself, then noticed Paltovis, Mewetesi, and Ikizuni approaching. They traversed a circular, thick glass tunnel flanked by guards at each end. The room Boprexu occupied was comfortably spacious but not excessively so, featuring a circular glass and metallic table designed for holographic communication, pending security clearance. A touchscreen embedded in the table facilitated weapons testing, managed by the team responsible for the city's operational integrity. Nonetheless, an override system was accessible to this team when necessary. The walls, transparent with black metallic vertical lines spaced inches apart, were adorned with images of Prime Architect Dekrehas and his wife. The metallic blue double doors, emblazoned with the Giyehe flag, sealed the room.

The three leaders entered, Paltovis at the forefront, radiating a commanding aura. Ikizuni, seemingly burdened by recent unsettling news, was almost alongside him. Mewetesi, with an unreadable expression, initially lagged behind but quickly caught up at the door. Boprexu pondered whether a fleeting thought had distracted her, yet she had regained her composure before the meeting commenced. He remained open to the possibility of being mistaken, awaiting the meeting's proceedings for further clarity.

The United Retaliation Force's leaders—officially named by the freedom fighters and unaffiliated leaders—were guided by the same visionary beings preparing the rebel factions to join the URF and unite in their struggle for liberation from the Yatavra-System Lords' tyranny.

Paltovis initiated the dialogue, "Mewetesi has expressed satisfaction with the progress in identifying new planetary systems for future Lutresas cities. Do you share this sentiment?"

Boprexu responded with measured optimism, "The Zatodex system harbours several planets suited for military and civilian settlements. Given our race's rapid breeding, we've always intended to bolster our numbers through cloning. Moreover, acquiring additional resources remains a priority. To date, I am content, especially hearing about the discovery of multiple systems meeting our requirements."

Mewetesi, barely concealing her enthusiasm, interjected, "I've explored planets in three systems, even setting foot on one and evaluating its mineral resources. This system, which we'll name Orgalax after the legendary Lutresas warrior, promises immense potential. Paltovis and I will personally oversee its defence, with support from some renegade fleets. Its security will demand a formidable fleet, including cruisers and carriers. Despite its distance, which is unprecedented in Lutresas exploration, we are fully prepared for this venture."

Ikizuni contributed, "Mocowas will find himself overextended if he attempts to confront our widespread operations. Our strategy is unfolding, and he stands no chance of averting his downfall should he engage us simultaneously. His response must be phased, allowing us to execute our plan, dispersing his forces and observing their dissolution. As he deliberates his military commitments, we'll dismantle his space force and target every Yatavra-dominated planet. Our objective is to compel the surrounding System Lords to recognize defeat and persuade Mocowas to surrender. While I prefer their complete eradication, I am open to any form of victory."

Turning to Paltovis, Boprexu inquired, "What about Ujesal and his fleet of new hunter cruisers? Their production is geared towards safeguarding Lutresa's interests and supporting an extensive war effort. The significant losses incurred by both sides have yet to be fully addressed, with reports of thousands of fighters perishing daily."

Paltovis replied, "We're producing hundreds of hunter cruisers daily, and pilots are readily available. We've already directed our forces to avoid patrolling certain regions of space teeming with enemy fighters. It's imprudent to squander pilots in conflicts over territories we cannot hope to govern. We must eschew needless skirmishes, focusing instead on sound strategies and providing our warriors with optimal directives, secure in the knowledge of our impending victory."

Mewetesi concurred enthusiastically, "Having experienced the chaos that ensues when pilots stray beyond their designated sectors, I can attest to the importance of adhering to our boundaries. We must not be lured into any snares. The enemy could exploit such distractions to orchestrate surprise assaults and capture critical areas in space, diverting our focus from safeguarding our essential assets."

Ikizuni agreed with a swift nod, "Indeed, it's only a matter of time before Mocowas, in a bid to assert his military supremacy, launches an onslaught with reckless abandon. The sacrifice of numerous pilots is of little consequence to him. His leadership is marked by folly and a lack of compassion."

Paltovis, speaking with evident disdain, added, "That much is clear. Should Mocowas find himself ensnared, he may attempt to breach our space defences, deploying his new fleet against our allied planets, especially those densely populated civilians. Yet, he's also aware that such aggression could turn public sentiment against him. As more races align with our cause, even those previously loyal to the System Lords might withdraw their support from a leader whose actions verge on genocide. The future will reveal the path we must take. The original scriptures foretold of this moment, and their words resonate anew with each utterance. Warriors will perish, and innocents will suffer until we emerge healed and liberated. Let us hold in our thoughts those who have fallen. My friends, the war that now commences will indelibly change us in myriad ways."

Chapter Thirty-One

Three hundred Yatavra military guards stood in the courtyard of Gorxab's residence on planet Kovenabi, situated in the Deveskali system, observing the grand lord master as he adjusted his red uniform blazer and black cloak. Mocowas had appointed Gorxab to the planet as the Grand Lord Master ten cycles ago for strategic purposes. Now, Gorxab found himself back in Kovenabi, a key hub situated at the nexus of several vital borders for the Yatavra and an essential trade route. Gorxab hadn't visited in six cycles, having quickly grown weary of the planet's entertainment options. Nonetheless, he had brought along a small contingent of Tekxedin males for companionship and females to provide pleasure and attend to his desires.

Gorxab's mission involved leveraging Hetkarej's expertise to secure the trade routes, ensure the smooth transit of supplies and protect the clone factories within the system, where elite hybrid warriors were forged for battle. Ralshafa, a specialist in space combat, welcomed this assignment, eager to demonstrate her capabilities to Mocowas beyond mere loyalty—traits the supreme System Lord had come to recognise.

Every System Lord played a pivotal role, and Gorxab was acutely aware of his significance. Mocowas intended to maximise Gorxab's potential, valuing his knack for dictatorship and strategic insight—a rare combination. Yet, Gorxab's tendency to shun confrontation, favouring escape over combat, was well-known. He understood that the troops and guards under his command were expressly tasked with quashing any opposition to their authority.

Having just enjoyed a sumptuous meal, Gorxab considered indulging further, enticed by the aroma of sweet fruit cakes and wine that filled the air as citizens celebrated the arrival of the formidable fleet. Gorxab's forces, complemented by Hetkarej's ground troops and an array of ships, had a pronounced presence in the system and its surroundings. Moreover, newly assembled, immensely powerful fleets stood ready in various systems, poised to secure emerging trade routes and fortify strongholds. These fleets, notable for their grandeur and lavish funding, were modelled after Gorxab's latest ships but on a grander scale. They were designed to transport extensive invasion forces to subdue enemy worlds.

The troops, parading in formation around Gorxab, captured the attention of local citizens, who observed from the seclusion of their brown, metallic-looking huts with slender walls. Though they remained indoors, they watched the military display through their windows. Kovenabi's inhabitants, primarily labourers transported off-planet for work, accepted their lot without question, offering unwavering support to the System Lords, the undisputed authority.

The streets were paved with dark grey stone, and the roads, brown and soiled, sprawled beneath a perpetually hot and humid climate—a condition Gorxab had grown accustomed to over his lifetime, despite the discomfort of donning Yatavra uniforms rather than the cooler gowns and robes preferred by many.

Gorxab's attention was drawn to the colossal military compound at the village's heart. The Yatavra strategically placed their compounds in secluded areas to shield their most formidable military members. While other System Lords favoured commanding from the capital cities—a practice criticized by strategists as tactically unsound—Gorxab chose to disregard the counsel he received, opting to visit the mountain base a few days hence.

Upon reaching the compound's entrance, Gorxab was greeted by Hetkarej and Ralshafa, both resplendent in their red uniforms. Their attire was meticulously crafted, with tailored trousers and blazers fastened up to the neck, their black cloaks billowing in the gentle breeze. Adorning the top left shoulder of their blazers was a singular black metal button encasing a small green gem. Gorxab himself bore three black metal buttons with a central white diamond, a distinction reserved for all Grand Lord Masters. Only Mocowas was distinguished by a gold button with a red diamond at its heart.

Gorxab found himself captivated by Ralshafa. He was well aware of the remarkable System Lord's past and her awareness of his insight. Ralshafa, once entangled in relationships with various male suitors, had grappled with feelings of alienation during her youth, questioning her gender identity. This internal conflict left her yearning for affection from both sexes. A confidante of Gorxab had safeguarded this secret, steering Ralshafa towards triumph and acclaim by moulding her to embody a dominant female Yatavra figure who dated men exclusively through sophisticated conditioning techniques. Though conflicted, Ralshafa found solace in a supportive circle, ensuring her secret remained with Gorxab. Despite Gorxab's reputation for debauchery, his royal status rendered him invaluable. Exposure to Ralshafa's personal life could have resulted in her undergoing harsh reconditioning by unyielding scientists, who reduced her to a mere test subject until deemed 'corrected.' Failure would have spelt her doom. The Yatavra, despite recognizing non-binary existence even among flawless clones, often showed disregard for such realities. Servants of the hierarchy were expected to adhere to a specific mould, with Gorxab being a notable exception. His open defiance and acceptance, even by disapproving System Lords, starkly contrasted with others who discreetly indulged with pleasure servants in what they deemed 'normal' interactions. Gorxab viewed these peers as hypocritical and judgmental.

As Hetkarej and Ralshafa moved aside, Gorxab observed their evident fatigue despite being engineered for resilience and vigour by top scientists. Even the finest required rest. Nonetheless, he was assured of their readiness for any scenario. The forthcoming discussion would test them all as they formulated a robust, practical strategy without compromising the fleet's defensive posture.

The compound, constructed from imposingly tall charcoal black stone, was cold and dark inside, with an almost smooth exterior. Its walls were embellished with tools for weapon manufacture, portraits of their inventors, and depictions of significant buildings in larger cities. Deeper within, holographic projections showcased past and present System Lords alongside busts of Mocowas, sculpted from specially blessed white stones akin to those used in sacred monuments. Gorxab couldn't suppress an eye roll upon encountering a room dominated by a statue of Mocowas, enthroned amidst skulls and crowns of conquered kings—a homage to his military conquests.

Following the guards who led the way, the three System Lords navigated past the compound's communication section to the operations rooms. One room, expansive and arranged with white desks and chairs at the back, featured a silver podium at the front, outfitted with sensors for transmitting messages to the planet's populace.

After the guards departed, Gorxab, Hetkarej, and Ralshafa took their seats. Gorxab, intent on cementing his legacy of success, announced, "I expect both of you to dedicate most of your time to managing the fleet. Henceforth, we shall minimize our presence on the planet. Our collective efforts must aim at securing a swift victory and the downfall of our adversaries. Mocowas has supplied us with ample ships to repel imminent threats, and only the foolhardy would dare penetrate so deep into enemy territory."

Hetkarej offered his perspective, "The truth is, the United Retaliation Force, as they're currently known, have assembled fleets of formidable ships equipped with advanced weaponry, significantly enhanced by Giyehe engineers. They're determined to eradicate us, bolstered by support from certain imperial rulers rallying behind the nations opposed to us."

Ralshafa outlined her approach, "We must draw the enemy to us before they considerably weaken us and our allies. Though potent as ours, the Ruduzen and Giyehe fleets lack our grandeur."

Gorxab shared his analysis, "The renegades aim to vanquish us in counterattacks after their substantial losses. Yet, they can ill afford the continuous loss of pilots and ships on such a scale. Presently, our manpower and fleet surpass theirs."

"Their vulnerabilities are evident; they will struggle to affect the core planets under our protection," Hetkarej added. "While some emperors remain supportive, others have retracted their backing, swayed by rumours concerning our conduct towards the Reduzen populace on Daheza. Regardless of these allegations, we are privy to the truth. Mocowas recently endorsed measures to isolate the Reduzen race, curtailing off-world communications."

Ralshafa weighed in, "Our military faces a formidable challenge. The renegades, comprising pirate scavengers and remnants of once-dreaded empires seeking resurgence, with allies contributing scholars, scientists, engineers, and military prowess, have solidified a nearly indomitable resolve."

Hetkarej nodded in agreement, "Ralshafa, your situation assessments are consistently precise. We'll capitalize on every opportunity to dismantle colonies sheltering dissenters. Any warlords who lend their support to our adversaries will meet their end. In the eyes of the System Lord council, those who offer us no utility are better eliminated."

Gorxab, with a smile, added, "That's an exemplary strategy, and should you succeed, Hetkarej, we'll all reap the benefits. Let's indulge in wine and fruit cake as we contemplate the rewards Mocowas will grant us after the war. I'm convinced you're destined for a supreme status. Pakowe will find it impossible to take credit for your plan, as you will implement it flawlessly and without a hitch. Not even the gods can impede your progress now."

Chapter Thirty-Two

Heturadi stood on the bridge of the Goliath; his gaze fixed on the planet below where new military bases, soon to double as training grounds for the next generation of intergalactic gladiator legions, were swiftly taking shape. He turned, a smile spreading across his face. The news from Emperor Oltexav and his military chiefs was promising; their joint forces were primed for conflict against the United Retaliation Force. This alliance signified a powerful ally with shared objectives, poised to join forces at the opportune moment to dismantle the Yatavra empire.

Aware of the formidable challenges ahead, Heturadi acknowledged the vital leverage an emperor's support could offer. Rumours circulated that Mocowas was devising a sinister scheme to obliterate all aligned with the United Retaliation Force, revealing his dawning realization of the significant opposition rallying against him.

Contemplating the scale necessary for a full-scale assault on all fronts, Heturadi concluded such an operation would be impractically expensive currently. The fleet commanders he faced were too shrewd and powerful to be defeated by brute force alone. His strategy would need to isolate each ally to prevent the united forces from regrouping after any offensive actions they initiated. Recognizing they likely harboured similar plans, he pondered which strategies would triumph. Heturadi considered the prospect of restless nights, tormented by the correctness of his decisions, before determining not to dwell on such concerns continuously during wartime.

Vedukraz, the chief strategist aboard the Goliath, had become Heturadi's source of innovative ideas and alternative tactics. Despite his reserved demeanour and the noticeable dark rash across his neck and part of his face, Vedukraz was amiable enough for someone who typically preferred solitude. He consistently made himself available to Heturadi, a Kalicos he had long respected throughout his esteemed career, ensuring he delivered his utmost in his presence.

Vedukraz, frequently sniffling, shared in his gravelly voice, "I am heartened to witness our military might expand daily, Fleet Commander Heturadi. The recruits are soon to arrive on planet Crosekol. The Borshux have granted us a locale to extend our formidable empire. Our ascendancy continues positively for our race. We've reached a point where engaging in numerous conflicts is imperative for our survival, all while keeping our focus on the ultimate goal: unmatched intergalactic supremacy. One day, we will diminish the riches of the Yatavra-System Lords to nothing as we subdue them and overhaul their civilization, instilling fear and suffering in their ranks."

"We must proceed with our planning carefully," Heturadi replied. "Our foes not only seek our defeat but dream of our annihilation as a race, resigned to subsist on the remnants they see fit to bestow upon us. I will not allow that to be the destiny of those I safeguard."

Vedukraz shook his head, "The Titan King's fury must be boundless. Disrespect has been hurled at him from every conceivable direction, challenging the dignity of a monarch of his stature." Heturadi expressed his disdain for the situation the king found himself in. "It appears that more than one titan empire is involved here, but only one truly matters. Grandres is the Titan King, and he will be the one to prove himself a worthy leader for the masses across every galaxy imaginable. I will ensure it."

"Masterful fleet commander, I am at your service for as long as you need me. I will aid in destroying the enemy. We have attackers and cruisers positioned near vital spaceports and space stations. Many of the new colonies are protected by our carrier ships, and the Borshux oversee the rest with part of their fleet. Mocowas has allocated fifteen thousand ships for assaults on smaller planets. He intends for the gladiator carriers to be used in invasions of many colonies where rebel leaders may be concealed. They are the primary supporters of the United Retaliation Force and the politicians who endorse them. These dissidents are why citizens on thousands of planets are now being detained, interrogated, and then transported to prison planets, which haven't been utilized to this extent for quite some time."

Heturadi frowned. "Mocowas must tread carefully to avoid provoking citizens on numerous planets. We do not need planet-scale rebellions in every galaxy."

Vedukraz responded, "The clone barons will dispatch large fleets of ships carrying Otrizon guards to many planets, as you know. The citizens of hundreds of nations under Yatavra control will be effectively regulated. The barons are commissioning clones around the clock, with factories being constructed rapidly and efficiently."

"Once the clone barons have control of the cities, our nations will easily overcome any difficulties we may encounter after defeating the System Lords. Now that Grandres has engaged with the Otrizon clone barons, everything is falling into place, and the leaders of both races agree. The chief baron, Mirehesa, concurs that the era of the Yatavra-System Lords is over. If they secure the systems and planets we promised, everything will proceed as planned. Mocowas's arrogant belief that he would dominate the clone barons will be his undoing."

"More challenges will arise for him, Fleet Commander Heturadi, so we must be prepared to support any action that eradicates the enemy. This will lighten our burden when confronting the System Lords for supreme control. We cannot afford to have our pilots and troops slaughtered by the forces we're combating while we attempt to usurp power from the System Lords. Everything will eventually fall into place, and then we will dictate who ascends and who is crushed beneath our feet."

Chapter Thirty-Three

A small convoy comprising six Yatavra cruisers and three carriers entered space above the planet Foreisa within the Esecrat system. A young captain stood on the bridge of one of the new cruisers, marked by its innovative, sleek wing design. The wings, sizeable and angled backwards, complemented the ship's main body, which was bulky with an almost peculiar long oval shape. However, its edges were sharply defined, rendering the vessel larger than a typical cruiser. Its design was unique, with curvature only at the ship's centre, where engineers and technicians were stationed. Engineered to rival the Reduzen hunter cruiser, this ship took a raw approach to armament, outfitted with an extensive arsenal of anti-gravity torpedoes, missiles, and laser cannons. These weapons were so densely packed in certain sections that they nearly concealed the ship's metallic frame. The armaments, arrayed above the bridge area and lining both sides of the hull and the bow tip, designated the vessel as a formidable destroyer of enemy ships. The captain nodded to the bridge's strategic crew, who engaged with the touchscreens before them, facilitating ship-to-ship communications. As the carrier bay doors opened, thirty-five attackers, merely a fraction of the close combat vessels aboard the carriers, descended toward the planet's surface. Their mission was to penetrate the defences of the capital city, Gotecas, where revolutionaries and retired rebel faction leaders convened to deliberate on recent developments that could alter the fate of numerous races across myriad galaxies.

Defensive systems, concealed beneath the terrain near the city's governmental buildings, sprang to life and locked onto the attackers, compelling them into evasive manoeuvres. Fighters, launched from beyond the capital's periphery, intercepted the attackers. Despite their high-tech, patchwork design, these fighters launched missiles targeting the buildings where discussions and communications with the URF regarding the assault were underway. Several towering edifices crumbled, entombing and claiming the lives of beings from diverse galaxies under the debris.

The fighters weaved between glass and metal towers, striving to evade collisions while acknowledging the inevitable city damage from shooting down the attackers. Despite the challenge of expelling the enemy from the city, they persevered. As they closely pursued, additional attackers entered from the sides, using evasive tactics to escape the fighters' line of sight. Sometimes, they darted outside city limits at incredible speeds before re-entering or executing barrel rolls to gain a tactical advantage. Then, they resumed firing on their targets within the city. As the initial group of attackers depleted their missile reserves, they turned their lasers on the scattering citizens. The diverse alien population reacted differently to the assault; some screamed under laser fire, while others, seasoned in warfare, sought cover silently. Military veterans among the aliens attempted to lead others to safety, directing them to underground bunkers where chaos ensued as citizens rushed for refuge. The attackers mercilessly targeted every visible citizen, while the fighters managed to down many enemy vessels in retaliation.

As the attackers' numbers diminished, they adopted a defensive stance. Reinforcements descended from space, launching missiles at still-occupied buildings, causing extensive damage and resulting in thousands of casualties. They fired through windows, eliminating nearly every citizen across various levels.

Fighters converged from the North, East, South, and West. Some even arrived from the base station on the ocean and the mountain bases guarding the mines against raiders of natural resource stocks. These fighters targeted the attackers, catching them from behind to the point where their vessels were damaged and deliberately crashed into buildings. Some tried to head towards the underground bunkers, which citizens were still entering. As fighters shot them out of the sky, several attacker pilots caused extensive casualties as they crashed in explosive heaps near the bunkers.

More attackers entered the city, gearing up for a final assault. The fighters encircled them but fired lasers through the window, using the burning buildings to cover the windows, eliminating a few alien beings at a time. The fighters closed in and unleashed their lasers, aiming to take down as many attackers as possible. Striking the attackers from behind and the side, the Yatavra close combat ships' pilots realized their mission was nearing its end. Despite initially underestimating the planet's defences, believing their attackers could withstand being outnumbered three to one by older close combat vessels, their arrogance was unfounded.

Upon reaching space, the attackers ascended out of the sky and docked with the carriers as swiftly as possible. The Yatavra cruisers and carriers then activated their hyper-light drive engines to vacate the space above the planet. Minutes after the Yatavra departure, eight renegade cruiser ships of various types arrived on the scene, summoned by the ground superiors the moment the attack on the political hub began. More ships followed, including several new Noxret and Jekaxtu carriers, echoing the design of their cruisers with massive hulls. This emerging retaliation force created fleets with a uniform design, a strategy Ikizuni and other commanders quickly decided. These ships had been relocating people from the planet, leaving none behind as their resources were still spread thin in some areas. Now, the planet will receive ample protection in the foreseeable future. The United Retaliation Force needed a strong presence wherever they had political and rebel support. Citizens rallied behind the rebels, openly expressing their disdain for the Yatavra empire across many planets. They faced total despair if left unprotected from the systematic slaughter ordered by the evil System Lords, rendering their suffering meaningless. This outcome was unacceptable. The struggle was set to alter lives profoundly, changing perceptions forever post-war. Even in the event of a loss, the freedom fighters' discourse of peace following victory remained their singular desire, instilling hope in every being rallying behind them.

Chapter Thirty-Four

Planet Akovatek was bustling as military troops engaged in combat training and manoeuvres on the extensive combat courses. Acres of military vessels filled the view, from sand cruisers and sky cruisers to converted sky carriers designed for longevity and durability under harsh conditions, with more powerful propulsion systems and heavier armour. The desert region of the planet hosted numerous pilots training in combat conditions, with certain battles reconstructed to mirror the experiences of the veterans mentoring them. The young pilots were rigorously tested, enduring pain as their bodies bore the marks of seatbelts from the forceful manoeuvres and high velocities. Being a Yatavra pilot was demanding, and the young, predominantly male, elite force was a testament to why so many had failed to conquer the Yatavra on the planets they ruled in the modern age.

The bases and compounds were heavily fortified, with cannon towers at every entrance and road leading to the camps where guards and troops resided and worked. Armed with laser rifles and guns, guards stood watch on tall towers or patrolled the dusty stone streets. Lookouts communicated regularly with the camps below. Troops conducted patrols, especially at night, when guards doubled until morning on Akovatek.

The space stations remained as busy as ever, with every superior fully aware of the Yatavra's war status. Close combat vessels patrolled the space around the planet despite the station and port commanders not anticipating attacks. With no recent activity in nearby systems and Akovatek's space station boasting an arsenal of new ships with massive destructive power, no commander expected an enemy force to venture near the planet or the adjacent systems in the Sezikal system.

The ports featured three long, diagonal white and red-coloured Xorillium metal tentacle-like docking bays extending from a massive red and grey sphere serving as the central command. Ships were aligned in rows, with larger vessels docked at the more expansive ports further down the bays and smaller ships arranged on either side of shorter ports. A secondary section of the space stations accommodated ships at long rectangular docks supported by numerous laser cannon stations. Hundreds of attackers patrolled far from the stations and ports, ready to respond if necessary.

The routine comings and goings at the spaceport and space stations kept the Yatavra from being overly anxious. Then, unexpectedly, thirteen Reduzen hunter cruisers and one hundred- and ten Star Ranger fighters emerged from hyper-light drive speed, directly into a patrol zone. The pilot of the leading Reduzen cruiser navigated to avoid colliding with the space station and ports while closing in on the patrol ships. When the

Reduzen starfighters and Yatavra attackers faced each other, they fired their laser cannons. Missiles struck the fronts of ships, causing many to spiral downwards and collide, their explosions merging into a massive fireball in space, resulting in instant death for many.

As Yatavra patrol ships clashed with Reduzen vessels, Lutresas cruisers and carriers emerged from the darkness of space at a distance. The Reduzen and Lutresas cruisers launched missiles and newly developed anti-gravity torpedoes, now standard on all United Retaliation Force vessels, targeting the ships docked at the spaceports. As this onslaught unfolded, more Star Ranger fighters darted into Yatavra space, their approach akin to predators emerging from the shadows into unknown territory, seeking another predator for sport. The space station suffered considerable damage as large metal fragments were torn from its tentacle-like structure, slicing many smaller ships in two and causing them to explode upon impact with the missiles. When these missiles struck the spaceport's debris, shards scattered in every direction, hitting attackers attempting to form a defensive line in front of the docked ships. These ships were nearly obliterated, their pilots panicking and screaming as the vacuum of space claimed them, their vessels torn apart and ejected into space, lifeless.

Rotumze fighters entered Yatavra space, their laser cannons blazing as they targeted the small ships attempting to escape the space station's docking areas for hyper-light drive speed. Following closely, Rotumze battle cruisers, several among the ten that arrived, released more fighters and attacked the small Yatavra ships joining the conflict. Over two hundred attackers were defending the space station, with hundreds more appearing. Their hyper-light drive engines halted, and they dived into nearby dogfights at top combat speed, exploiting the fact that many ships they aimed to destroy were targeting those docked at the spaceports.

Preventing these ships from joining the fray was a priority for the United Retaliation Force.

The allied fleets unleashed missiles at the port's central sphere. The enemy attackers, eager to see their foes perish in their ships, recognized the threat posed and did everything to protect themselves. They split into groups, hunting in packs, shooting down every fighter and drawing the attention of the Reduzen cruiser's cannon operators. Engaging in dogfights at incredible speeds, the Yatavra attackers drew close to the Reduzen cruiser cannons, making it difficult for the operators to target them. Then, additional attackers launched missiles at the Reduzen hunter cruiser, disabling its laser cannon, allowing them to fire at the fighters ruthlessly.

More attackers emerged from behind the space station as Lutresas cruisers concentrated their plasma torpedo fire on the formidable Akovatek space station. Unleashing their arsenal simultaneously, the attackers aligned in four staggered lines, with the first two lines surging forward while the last two split to the right and left, aiming to inflict maximum damage with their missiles before dispersing to disable the Lutresas cruisers' laser cannons. The rear lines rained down on their targets like a deluge, with most space fighters at that moment solely focused on eliminating Yatavra attackers.

Hecazy and Lutresas fighters arrived solely intending to target the smaller ships detaching from the spaceport docking area and shooting fighters out of the sky. Only a few small cruisers remained, scattered in pockets. At the same time, the passenger carrier ships fled the area using their hyper-light drive engines. The Hecazy fighters targeted ships at one end of the remaining metallic tentacles. In contrast, the Lutresas targeted ships at the opposite end, firing missiles at them as they disengaged, striking them on the hull's side or head-on as they manoeuvred tactically to evade incoming missiles and laser fire. The small Yatavra cruisers sustained heavy damage, with some pilots losing control, leading their vessels to drift aimlessly in space, some colliding with the space station and exploding or being hit by missile fire as they altered course.

The task of eradicating the entire space force above planet Akovatek was still in view. Still, the allied fleets needed to act swiftly. Every free cruiser fired upon Yatavra battle cruisers that had managed to break free from the docking bays and were opening their bay doors to release their attackers. The missiles obliterated more than half of the attackers that the carriers had onboard as they were emerging. The remainder of the attackers then found themselves under a barrage of laser fire from Lutresas fighters.

The attackers quickly adapted their combat style, attempting to navigate through the debris of the exploding space station. Yet, many were unsuccessful and crashed into metal fragments from ship hulls destroyed by enemy fire. Despite skilled pilots executing numerous intricate manoeuvres on both sides, the cruisers efficiently targeted many of the attackers as they performed half-barrel rolls while navigating the challenging debris field. The attackers sought to evade being hit, but additional fighters arrived and swiftly eliminated them.

With most, if not all, attackers neutralized, the focus shifted to bombing. This phase was initiated promptly, with twenty-eight Giyehe cruisers arriving in under three minutes. The anticipation of more attackers loomed. Despite over seven hundred enemy pilots being defeated, reinforcements were expected. The territorial scatter bombs, soon to be a staple in nearly every United Retaliation Force ship's arsenal with their highly effective design, were deployed by the Giyehe cruisers orbiting above the planet. As they opened their bomb bay doors, they released their payload over the camps, which had been blaring sirens throughout the space conflict. The bombardment substantially damaged the compounds, military vehicles, and equipment. While many troops were sheltered underground, countless others remained on the surface, ready for a potential invasion.

The impact of the bombs significantly altered the landscape above the bunkers, yet the troops maintained silence. The explosive force sent ground-shaking shockwaves across the military training area, resulting in the widespread destruction of ground vessels. The sonic blasts deafened any troops above ground before shrapnel tore through them or the shockwaves inflicted fatal wounds. The bombs' force threw Yatavra guards to the ground, raising clouds of dust that made breathing difficult, and even solidified dirt became lethal debris that flayed the skin from the enemies' faces. Through this relentless assault, the Giyehe aimed to convey their determination to triumph in the war, regardless of its duration or brutality.

Chapter Thirty-Five

Mocowas seethed as he stood on the balcony of his beach residence near the ocean. The supreme commander's anger surged uncontrollably as he reflected on the recent attack on Akovatek and other concerns. It was evident that more ships needed to be deployed in space. Despite his strategists' belief that the Yatavra's heavily guarded stations and ships were secure, the unexpected and bold attack on Akovatek had proven otherwise. This strike, targeting a strategically vital space station and one of the Yatavra's crowning achievements, had long-term implications visible to all System Lords and their military experts. Mocowas reminisced about his awe upon first witnessing the Akovatek space station, home to one of the largest vessels he had ever seen. A colossal new space station was under construction in the Wetrasan system, promising to be an even more remarkable sight.

Despite facing significant challenges, Mocowas remained resolute in expanding his empire.

Rebels increasingly joined the United Retaliation Force, including reclusive but powerful leaders from the Noxret and the Xumewes race, who had parted ways with the Lutresas many cycles ago under King Vadagul's reign. They sought strong alliances with the United Retaliation Force, posing a significant threat to the Yatavra, of which Mocowas was acutely aware. The war's direction was shifting, necessitating major strategic adjustments for Mocowas to achieve his desired outcomes. Rather than offering relief, the cool breeze on his face only fueled his anger, particularly as he struggled to enjoy the typically hot Etrehen summers during such turbulent times.

Reflecting further on the war, Mocowas considered those significantly impacting the Yatavra-System Lords' position. The United Retaliation Force's attacks on numerous colonies had already made a mark, challenging the search for more leaders among old allies who once commanded large followings as freedom fighters and rebels. Ralshafa, in particular, had made significant progress, successfully attacking key targets and discovering two secret moon bases. Although many prisoners were taken, including two lower-level Hecazy base commanders, the lack of knowledge about an important meeting location led to their torture and death by the Yatavra, unable to extract information the commanders did not possess. Ralshafa's indifference to the fate of prisoners of war suggested to Mocowas that she would become an effective fleet commander. He also harboured high expectations for Esekal, believing she would become a formidable adversary for the enemy. Mocowas yearned for results that would critically weaken the United Retaliation Force's defensive line, as this was the only outcome that would truly satisfy him.

Chapter Thirty-Six

The Giyehe military command centre on Epeyi had been constructed with remarkable skill and rapidity. Its design intentionally gave the military base a formidable appearance, with an almost crooked look to its angles when viewed from above. The tall pillars, made of shiny black metal, ended in high, pointy spirals that seemed to stretch indefinitely. Around the base, underground launch bays and launchpads near the watchtowers accommodated ships.

Dekrehas was in the base's spacious holo-chamber, which featured five levels where a superior could stand, surrounded by multiple sensors. Floating panels projected the images of Fasjey, Ikizuni, Mewetesi, and Jarkepe around the room. They were about to commence a mandatory meeting, a regular occurrence given the constant influx of new information. Sometimes, confronting the death toll on other planets was overwhelming, requiring Dekrehas to reflect. Nevertheless, he remained committed to utilizing his expertise to support the United Retaliation Force's victory in the war.

Dekrehas had managed not to let the war consume him, thanks largely to his wife, Tadrashi, for her steadfast support in preventing him from succumbing to stress.

Ikizuni, always prepared for battle, was the first to speak, emphasizing the urgent need for more ships. "Empress Cesukrex has assured me that her fleets will be available, with ships dispatched to every necessary system. The planets that have been bombarded will receive ample protection. The Yatavra military's next objective is to conquer entire planetary systems where citizens have become rebellious, aiming to bolster their troop presence on the ground. Meanwhile, we're also focused on constructing as many ships as possible at our shipyards. Having lost over fifty thousand Giyehe ships, we're not even halfway through a war cycle. These challenging times were expected. The space above the planet and within this system has never been busier."

Ikizuni then pondered the impact of their actions on Akovatek, acknowledging the nerve struck within the Yatavra troops.

Fasjey, with a grin, suggested, "We're all seasoned in warfare. I propose we heed Jarkepe's advice and carefully consider our next steps."

Jarkepe quickly added, "Mocowas will seek to gain more territory, and we must counteract. Oshdan and I have crafted a strategy to enhance support for the rebels on Yatavra-controlled planets. Their vast size makes them challenging to govern, and even with significant support from Empress Cesukrex and our new ally, Emperor Drajulson, controlling the populace remains difficult. We're currently not doing enough. I plan to deploy ground support to the desert rebels from the Rotumze and

Hecazy races across multiple planets. They will dismantle the enemy, but swift action is imperative."

Dekrehas responded, "Proceed as you deem necessary. Escalating support for the rebels is the logical next step. You'll have access to all required resources and finances. While many warlords and factory barons may shun us, we have numerous alternatives."

Mewetesi interjected, "That's the essence of war. With the right currency, there's no shortage of lords and tyrants willing to sell military arms to a nation."

Fasjey then addressed Mewetesi, "We desperately need financial support. I'm currently engaging with all the queens who admire our efforts, and I am confident in securing the backing of several. They've opposed the Yatavra in any forthcoming power struggle, advocating for a new intergalactic political system. They were receptive to what Dekrehas and I communicated in our last broadcast to every reachable galaxy. I'll keep you updated," Fasjey announced.

Dekrehas nodded in response. "There is something we will have to learn, even though we know the process well, and that is how to link up with possible allies faster than before so that the United Retaliation Force can truly grow. We must prove we can protect those who fight alongside us to achieve the right results. This revolution is fought by leaders and warriors who will not accept failure when success and victory are possible and are the only outcomes they work towards." Dekrehas looked into the eyes of all the superiors around him and could see how much his words had registered with them. They understood what needed to be done and would fight hard to bring about a new era of calm that would resolve the problems of other nations for many cycles to come for the sake of all the races that needed to be saved. But first, the war needed to be won, and that would be the toughest challenge he and his allies were ever likely to face in their lifetime. Time was not on their side, and each cycle they fought brought about more death and destruction. Dekrehas would have to use all his knowledge and experience to navigate the journey ahead. He was determined to see it through to the end.

Tshekedi Wallace

TIMELINE
AFTER THE DESTITUTE ERA (A.D.E)

MAIN CHARACTERS

KALICOS RACE
King Grandres Volaxi
Prince Veleskin Volaxi
General Vatemfa
Fleet Commander Heturadi
Pakavet Kings Intergalatic Gladiator Guard Trainer and Mentor
Emwefi Royal Court Advisor
Anfeku Second Royal Court Advisor

REDUZEN RACE
Queen Fasjey Orunvo
General Jarkepe
Fleet Commander Ujesal
Beast Master Oshdan
Ruyey Queens Confidant
Yelesu Queens Advisor
Iklas Queens Advisor
Srankat, Head of The Queens Guard

YATAVRA RACE
Supreme Lord Master Mocowas
Grand Lord Mistress Esekal
Grand Lord Master Pakowe
Grand Lord Master Gotab Jowekre
System Lord Master Hetkarej
System Lord Ralshafa

MORTARSA RACE
Fleet Commander Elazret

GIYEHE RACE
Prime Architect Dekrehas
General Wesyal
Fleet Commander Paltovis
Tadrishi
Razce, at Top Architect and Politician
Katseu Labour Minister

BORSHUX RACE
Fleet Operations Master Sorzikel

OTRIZON RACE (CLONE BARONS)
Head Baron Mirehesa
Chief Scientist Feyesma
Baron Vinektel

LUTRESAS RACE
Queen Xunaseta
Alpha Guardian Boprexu
Fleet Commander Mewetesi Yosuntuk

RENEGADE FORCE LEADERS

JEKAXTU RACE
Captain/Fleet Commander Ikizuni

ROTUMZE RACE
Second Fleet Commander Letroxi
Captain Asutex

NOXRET RACE
Captain Redejanto

HECAZY RACE
Captain Tucawaz

DEAD CHARACTERS
Supreme lord Master Nesrodrel
Yatavra Legend from the destitute era.
Supreme Lord Master Valazon
Last Yatavra Supreme lord Master to serve a king.
King Dowalez
Father of King Grandres.
Ascalo
Hetkarej's father and the name of one of his legendary forefathers.

CREATURES

Tethaza Beast
Looks like a gigantic lion black with a thick red horn on the head and large white tusks in the bottom of the mouth with sharp ends.

Oroyes Serpent
Crimson-coloured gargantuan snake.

Jawanga Beast
It was a large, bright orange bear-looking beast with a horn sticking out of its head and chin and jagged, crooked teeth.

Grapahi Worms
Long white worms with big pink blotches on them.

Jerefi Spider
Orange body with brown spots and black legs. Lays grey eggs.

Reweska Sea Serpent
It is a twenty-foot-long yellow/green sea serpent with two large, sharp, fang-like teeth that show outside its mouth.

Orekesi Beast
A rider can use this ten-foot beast with hardened black skin, red eyes, and large roundish heads with an odd, shaped bone structure that looks like small formations of bumps next to their ears. They have a short brown snout with gnarling sharp teeth and stand ten feet tall on four legs with wide hoofs and brown hair around them.

Vetacav
Boar-like creature with white skin and a blue/grey underbelly

Kowoyiz Lizard
Long red large lizard with dark blue oval eyes and long, hard-skinned tail.

Jujowek fish
Red and yellow with blue dots on their tails, sharp teeth and black eyes.

Barukath
Eleven-foot beasts with skin-like leather that walk on two legs have fang-like teeth with paws and sharp claws on which they walk and at the end of their long gangly arms.

Pathrak
Black Scaled skin, six-legged creature with big bones.

MAIN PLANETS, PLANETARY SYSTEMS, STAR SYSTEMS AND NEBULAS

Locask system
Giyede has secret shipyards and space dock stations in abundance.

Eregahi
Planet where otekesi beasts come from.

Ketewdi system
Yatavra owned system where ships are built.

Hortrax system
Mortarsa spaceport.

Radarek system
Mortarsa spaceport.

Netartra nebula
Close to Lutresa's home planet.

Jekosei nebula
Near the Giyede home planet.

Qusoki
Lutresas home world

Gukazut
Jekaxtu home world.

Otreven
Borshux home world.

Planet Pesdrokar
Desert planet and home to the Kowoyiz lizard.

Esyoret
The planet where the Hoyatan race lives.

Kretaq
Giyehe homeworld.

Rasodorn
Clone Baron's home world.

Etrehen
Yatavra home world

Planet Hawtokax
Mocowas is a private planet.

Keshiwen system.
Mocowas planetary system.

Zatodex system
The planetary system was once owned by the clone barons.

Rakashaje
Wasteland planets were once owned by the Takrezac warlords.

Yewose nebula
This nebula is near the Zatodex system, where the Lutresas war breeder's factories, which were once owned by the clone barons, are.

Wetrasan system
Yatavra is building a Colossus spaceport this system.

Milton Keynes UK
Ingram Content Group UK Ltd.
UKHW050133270624
444593UK00006BA/97

9 781988 680477